My
FAKE BAD
Boyfriend

A
HOT UNDER THE MISTLETOE
ROMANCE

SARA WHITNEY

My Fake Bad Boyfriend: A Hot Holiday Novella

Ebook ISBN: 978-1-953565-10-5
Print ISBN: 978-1-953565-17-4

First Edition: November 2021
v. 1.7

To the Disco Vinnie fans.

And to MJ, always, for all the things.

Wanted:
One very bad boyfriend for the holidays

I don't just need a fake boyfriend. I need the worst fake boyfriend in the world. Someone who'll get my family off my back about my perpetually single state. Someone so awful they'll beg me to never bring another man home again.

Gabe promised he was up to the task, but by the time we've said hello to the parents and dropped our bags in my childhood bedroom, I've learned that he's a little *too* good at being bad.

We have so much fun, in fact, that I start to forget it's all for show.

By the time Christmas Eve rolls around, Gabe's the only thing I want to unwrap. And if I do, I'm afraid he'll be the gift I never want to return.

Keep in touch!

CHAPTER ONE

Darby

I'm overdressed. Or maybe I'm underdressed. What should a person wear to meet her fake boyfriend?

If it's brown wool tights, I'm all set for this stupid, embarrassing meet-up.

Every time the heavy door to the Beaucoeur Public Library creaks open, I whip my head in that direction. My work day ended twenty minutes ago, so I'm hovering at the edge of children's fiction, trying to act nonchalant. The bright December sun sears my eyes as the door swings shut, but each time it's not the person I'm waiting for. Not that I know what the person I'm waiting for looks like, but I'm pretty sure he's not a stressed-out mom of three or an eighty-year-old man with a walker.

Oh God, what if he's the eighty-year-old man with a walker?

I'm losing my nerve. Why did I let Faith talk me into

this? It started off as a joke, but somehow it ballooned into *this*.

I grab my phone to text her that I'm calling it off when the door opens one more time and a tall figure blots out the sun. I'm still a little dazzled as the door swings shut and the man's eyes sweep across the main library room. I'm guessing he's doing the same calculus I've done, dismissing the frazzled mother, the old guy unloading his returns onto the wooden counter, and my bald boss Ron, bent over the computer at the main desk.

Then his eyes land on me, and his expression shifts from focused to friendly as he heads in my direction.

My palms are sweating. I scrub them along the sides of my corduroy skirt, aware that I'm going to have to shake his hand. Wait, do people still shake hands? Isn't that considered a hygienic no-no now? What do you say to the person who's going to be sharing a bathroom with you at the end of the month if everything goes right?

"Darby St. Claire?"

Guh. His voice is deep, and although he's smiling at me as he tucks his knit hat into the pocket of his Carhartt jacket, he doesn't extend his hand to shake. Looks like he feels the same way I do about unnecessary germs. Oh hell, maybe he doesn't like touching *at all*.

Wait, that's probably for the best given the circumstances.

He's looking at me expectantly, his hands tucked into the back pockets of his jeans, and I still haven't said anything. Double hell. I offer my best smile, which probably looks frighteningly perky, and tuck my hair behind my ear.

"Hi!" I clear my throat and try again, slightly more controlled this time. "Yeah, that's me. You're Gabe?"

Gabe Dickenson. Faith hadn't told me what he looked like, just that I wouldn't be disappointed.

She was correct. This handsome man who smells like cold air and pine trees is waiting for me to take the lead on this meeting while I'm standing here staring at his shoulders. His beautiful broad shoulders.

"Thanks for meeting me here," I finally say, my voice sounding abnormally stiff.

He glances over his shoulder at the checkout desk, then looks back at me. "Are they going to shush us?" His voice drops to a whisper. "Are we even allowed to talk?"

This gives me pause. "Have you never been to a library? You're allowed to talk."

A frown, there and gone, passes over his face. Great, I've already managed to offend him. "Not that I think it's bad if you haven't—"

"Faith said you have a proposition for me." He's still smiling, but it's less relaxed now.

Okay then. Now I'm the one looking over my shoulder at the checkout desk. The old guy is sorting through his return pile as Ron patiently waits, his watchful gaze sweeping the main library floor.

"Follow me." I jerk my head to the right and Gabe shrugs and lets me lead him past Sendak and Seuss and Silverstein until we reach the end of the children's section and turn right, heading deep into adult periodicals. So much of it's online now that this section doesn't see much traffic, which means we should be able to talk without bothering anybody or being overheard. I'd rather die than have that last thing happen.

We both take a seat in the periodicals reading nook, and he shrugs out of his coat and leans back in his chair, propping his ankle on his knee and slinging his arm over the chair back. His jeans look comfortably worn and his boots are scraped and dirty, clearly for work and not for show. When the sleeve of his gray Henley pushes slightly up his wrist, I see the edges of a tattoo peeking under the cuff.

I swallow again. This was a bad idea.

"This was a bad idea."

I don't usually say exactly what I'm thinking, but expediency seems important at this point.

"You say that like you've never hired a boyfriend before." Every time he smiles, the corners of his eyes crinkle. It's a distraction. So is his messy dark hair and his tall, lean body. He's not at all who I'd pick as my boyfriend. He's not even somebody I'd stand next to at a bar while I was trying to catch the server's eye. He's too... scruffily attractive. Too confident. Too unaccustomed to libraries and the whole librarian lifestyle. Well, *my* librarian lifestyle anyway. Plenty of my cohorts are the cool types who never stay in on a Saturday night.

I lace my fingers together in my lap, feeling strung as tight as a drum in the face of his loose-limbed sprawl. "I haven't. Obviously. Have you, um..."

"Been an escort before?"

Alarm bells jangle through me. "An escort?" My voice is a little screechy, and he throws his head back with a burst of laughter that Ron definitely heard up at the front. Oh God.

He must see me starting to panic because he leans forward and rests an elbow on his knee. I get a glimpse of even more of his tattoo now, and it looks like it covers a chunk of his forearm.

"Bad choice of words," he says. "Look, Faith said you need a guy to take home for Christmas to get your parents off your back, but I'm not an escort." He crosses his arms over his chest, his lips quirked in amusement. "That means I'm not going to sleep with you, no matter how much you beg."

"I wasn't asking you to..." My voice drops to a whisper even though we're still alone. "We won't even be sharing a bedroom. This isn't about sex."

"Good, because I'd have to report you to the authorities for propositioning me. Solicitation's illegal, you know."

He's dead serious now, and I press my hands to my flaming cheeks as I shoot to my feet. "You should go. This was a —"

"Darbs, I'm kidding." He's laughing now and gesturing at my chair. "I'm sorry. Please sit."

I drop like a puppet whose strings have been cut, trying to get a read on this guy who's got me so off-balance so quickly. We've been talking for what, five minutes? And he's already shortened my name and jokingly threatened to have me prosecuted. It's way too much for me.

Maybe he senses that he's pushed me too far because when he speaks again, it's in a soothing, *calm the startled deer who's about to bolt* tone.

"I don't know how much Faith told you, but I don't have family in the area"—another quicksilver frown—"so it's not like I have anywhere to go for Christmas. She thought I might be able to help you out. That's it."

"And you've never done the pretend boyfriend thing before?"

He slumps in his chair and laces his fingers behind his head. "Do I *look* like a Hallmark movie dude?"

Actually, yes. He looks like the small-town boyfriend who owns a Christmas tree farm and is waiting to steal me away from the big-town lawyer fiancé who takes me for granted. Then again if I had a neglectful lawyer fiancé, we wouldn't be here. My mom would swoon over a lawyer, even if he was a big-city asshole.

Gabe fidgets in his seat, his fingers tapping the arm of his chair.

"Okay, so let's talk about what you need from me." His hands are big, like the rest of him, and I bet that Christmas tree farmer's boots look a lot like his do. "I can be polite to your mom and talk sports with your dad. I can eat overcooked turkey and compliment the decor and play nice with your tipsy aunt. I'll even hold your hand and look at you like you're the only woman in the world if that would help."

His face is warm and open as he studies me, and if this is a glimpse at how he'd act as a fake boyfriend, I'm a little worried that I'll be the one swooning. And my mom? God, she'll be ecstatic. In fact, I almost hate to give my family the satisfaction of bringing home such a quality boyfriend after all those years of "joking" harassment about my singleness.

Gabe's smiling as he waits for me to respond, but I'm caught in that last thought so long that he raises his brows in a question. "Darby? Is that what you're looking for? Because I'm happy to—"

"New plan."

I blurt it out, surprising both of us. He leans back and waits for me to speak, and I say the wild, stupid thing that just popped into my head.

"I don't need you to be the world's best boyfriend. I need you to be the world's worst one. Can you do that?"

CHAPTER TWO

Gabe

"Come again?"

The blushing brunette perched on the chair across from me just threw a wild curveball. I agreed to meet her because I was curious about the kind of woman who'd want to bring a stranger with her to her family's Christmas. But now that I've met her, I'm invested. Plus, I want to hold my fingers to her cheeks to see if that flushed skin is hot to the touch, but she's so jumpy that it would probably send her catapulting through the nearest window. So I keep my hands to myself and wait for her to explain the latest wrinkle in this already unhinged meeting.

"I need you to be the worst boyfriend you can possibly be."

"Why the hell would you want that?"

She bites her lip, sinking her teeth into the plump

redness that already lured me into joking about being an escort, then tries to explain her leap in logic.

"I just can't take it anymore. 'Oh Darby, still no boyfriend? Aren't you lonely?' 'Oh Darby, maybe if you read less, you'd find someone.' 'Oh Darby, I met the nicest man at the dentist's office. I'd love to introduce you.'" She shifts in irritation, the wooden chair creaking under what I've already observed is a hot little ass. "That nice man was the actual dentist by the way."

She looks at me in outrage, and I play my part. "No way."

"I know! He's fifty years old and he roots around in other people's mouths for a living, and my mom thinks he's perfect for her daughter." She huffs a little. "I just can't take another holiday of everybody in my family ganging up on me, but at the same time, I kind of want to..."

She waves her hands in silent frustration, so I finish her thought for her.

"Punish them?"

"Exactly!"

Now she's got her arms folded over her chest almost defensively, and I struggle to hold back my smile. Her plan, if I'm starting to understand what she's thinking, is diabolical. "So you want me to be the worst possible boyfriend for a week, so when you dump me, they beg you to never bring another person back with you for the holidays?"

She grins. "Do you think you can pull off being a bad boyfriend for a couple of days?"

Things suddenly aren't quite as amusing. "Do you want emotionally distant? Sexually selfish? Unambitious and drinking too much? Because those, I've done."

Her pretty mouth drops open, and I realize I've been a tad too honest.

"Ha," I say quickly. "Joking. I'm not that guy anymore." Thank God. Me today would kick nineteen-year-old me's ass. That guy sucked, and every girl who broke up with him was right to do it.

But Darby looks thoughtful. "Those aren't terrible ideas, actually."

"No." I say it quickly, but I don't ever want to be that aimless, angry guy again. "I can be a much better bad boyfriend than that. Let's see... I can spoil the ending of every movie your family brings up while I'm there. I can hit on your sisters. I can derail the Christmas dinner conversation by explaining that birds aren't real. I can—"

"Wait." Darby makes a buzzer sound and holds her hand up. "Birds aren't real?"

"Definitely not," I say. "They're battery-operated government drones. You see—"

Another buzzer sound, but it trails off in a giggle. "Save it for Christmas dinner. That's great."

She rests her hand on her chest, her slim fingers fluttering at the base of her throat. She's wearing a fuzzy white sweater, and I can't stop thinking about running my hands over it to see if it's as soft as it looks. Is there any way I can ask her to pack it for our week together?

"What else?" she asks.

I tip my head to the ceiling, back on task. "Whatever political persuasion your parents are, I can take the opposite position."

She snorts softly, then claps her hand over her mouth. This is a woman who needs to snort-laugh more.

"So what should we say you do for work?"

I shoot her a grin. "I'm a dentist, actually."

Her eyes widen and then drop to my wrist. She's looking at my ink and clearly trying to reconcile the dentist life with the tattoo life. I cluck my tongue over her lack of imagination. When she starts to stutter an apology, I can't hold back my laugh anymore. "I'm fucking with you. But you know, they let dentists get tattoos."

More pink in her cheeks, but at least she's laughing along this time. "Okay, so we're not going with the dentist thing. What should we say?"

I shrug. "I'll tell them I got my GED this spring, and I'm hoping to open a landscaping business with my friend Jonesy next year."

She beams at me. "That's perfect! Oh, my mother will *hate* that."

Well, isn't that a bucket of cold fucking water.

"Cool," I say stiffly. "Glad she won't approve."

Darby's still chuckling as she flips her hair over her shoulder. "So what do you do really? Faith didn't say."

"I got my GED this spring, and I'm hoping to open a landscaping business with my friend Jonesy next year." I meet her gaze, and this time her blush isn't as cute.

"I... I'm so sorry. I didn't mean..."

I wave a dismissive hand, even though I know the sting of her amusement will sit with me for a little bit. "It's okay. No self-respecting adult has a friend named Jonesy."

She laughs a little, but it's not like before, and Christ, now I feel bad that she feels bad.

"Hey, would you rather see if Jonesy wants to be your fake boyfriend? I can give him a call." When I stand to pull my phone from my pocket, her eyes take their time traveling down my body. Interesting. Does the fuzzy-sweatered librarian like what she sees?

"That's okay," she says quickly. "Better the devil you know."

"Devil? I can get a little naughty, if that's what you want," I say with a wink.

I didn't mean that to sound quite so sexual, but when Darby's breath hitches in her chest, it stops my breath too, knowing my words affected her like that.

I recover first.

"So what else do you need from me for Christmas with the St. Claire clan? Do you need a boring know-it-all who dominates every conversation he gets into?"

"I assumed that was the plan, given our time together so far."

She blinks at me, a vision of pure innocence, and it takes a second for me to realize that she's the one fucking with me now.

"Careful what you wish for," I warn her. "Do you know how many varieties of flowering shrubs thrive in the central Illinois hardiness zone? Because I do, and I'll list them all."

She laughs softly. "Impressive." Then she turns serious again. "So, um, my parents live just outside of Chicago, and I'm planning on getting there December twenty-first and staying through the twenty-seventh. Would you be available that long?"

I nod. "Not a lot of landscaping jobs in December."

"Okay," she says. Then she takes a deep breath, her shoulders rising and falling under that damn sweater. "I guess we need to talk about your payment."

"My payment?" Okay, now I do feel a little like an escort. "Faith kind of presented this as a favor to a friend."

Faith actually presented it as a favor to a sweet people-pleasing friend who was incapable of telling her overbearing parents to butt out of her life, and since I know a thing or two about family conflict and didn't have any particular plans for the holidays, I agreed to meet this woman out of curiosity. And now that I know she's cute and funny and blushes easily, I'm glad I did.

"I can't ask you to give up your whole Christmas to hang out with a bunch of strangers for free." She presses her lips together and runs her hands over the tops of her thighs. Both of those activities are highly distracting, and I force myself to focus on what she's saying.

The thing is, I don't need the money. I mean, I'm opening a business, so I always need money. But the amount I could reasonably ask for something like this is a drop in the bucket when it comes to the small business loan Jonesy and I are in the process of securing. Then again, it feels a little pathetic to just do this for free even though it's a huge relief not to spend the holidays alone again.

Inspiration strikes. "Any chance you own your own house?"

She nods.

"Any chance that house needs some landscaping work?"

"Yes." She's grinning now; maybe she felt as weird about offering me money as I felt about taking it. "I'd be delighted to hire Hot Guys Landscaping LLC to do some work once you're up and running."

I sling myself back against the chair, twisting my mouth into a confident smirk. "How'd you know that's what we're calling it?"

Her laugh is embarrassed, and it heats my blood. Cute librarian Darby thinking I'm hot makes everything about this deal more interesting.

"Okay then. You've got a fake bad boyfriend for the holidays." I stand. Stretch. Sitting still for too long makes me antsy. When I raise my arms, Darby's eyes focus on the slice of exposed skin between my jeans and the hem of my shirt.

That's when I decide that I want to learn more about this woman.

"Here." I grab my phone, unlock it, and hand it to her. "Put your number in. I may need to text you for inspiration as I work on my character."

She glances up from where she's typing in my phone. "Your character? So professional."

"You're going to hire me to plant every flowering bush in the 5b zone." I grin at her as I take the phone back. "I'm planning to earn it."

CHAPTER THREE

Nineteen days before departure:

> **GABE**
> What teams do your parents root for?

> **DARBY**
> The Cubs and the Bears, obviously.

> **GABE**
> Okay.

Sixteen days before departure:

> **GABE**
> What's your type?

> **DARBY**
> O negative?

GABE

Cute. I mean the type of guy you usually date.

DARBY

This is an impossible question.

GABE

???

DARBY

I don't date much, okay? But I guess smart guys. Professionals. Lots of wine bars and tickets to the symphony until they get too busy to call me back.

GABE

Still better than a dentist.

DARBY

Say it again for the people in the back.

Fifteen days before departure:

DARBY

We get dressed up for Christmas Eve dinner. Is that okay?

GABE

Like tuxedos?

DARBY

Like dresses and button-down shirts with ties. Absolutely no jeans.

GABE

Okay, I'll pack my fanciest party dress.

Twelve days before departure:

GABE

How do you feel about mustaches?

DARBY

I hate them.

GABE

Cool. I have a week and a half to grow one and offer your mother mustache rides every time we're alone.

DARBY

No

GABE

No mustache rides. Got it.

DARBY

NOTHING WITH MY MOTHER.

GABE

Your mother? Here I was thinking she was your older sister.

DARBY

The deal is off.

Nine days before departure:

DARBY

Sorry I missed your call. Hit you back tomorrow?

GABE

Sure.

So are you out tonight? Hot date? WAIT, ARE YOU CHEATING ON ME, YOUR TERRIBLE BOYFRIEND?

DARBY

Yes, I'm cheating on you with three other women. We're drinking wine and wrapping Christmas gifts tonight.

GABE

And having sexy pillow fights, right?

Tell me there are pillow fights, Darbs. I need this fantasy if you're going to ignore my calls.

Mmmm, fluffy pillows.

DARBY

You are seriously disturbed.

Six days before departure:

GABE

When are you sending the itinerary?

DARBY

What itinerary?

GABE

Does your family not have a Christmas itinerary?

DARBY

Um, no.

Wait, does yours?

Oh my God, this explains so much about you.

GABE

Forget I asked.

DARBY

No way. I'm going to make an itinerary just to put "Darby introduces new boyfriend to family" on it.

GABE

Is that before or after "Darby tells her family that Gabe is the world's greatest lover?"

DARBY

Before, obviously.

GABE

Okay. I'll pencil it in for next week.

Four days before departure:

DARBY

Okay, so my brother managed to change his holiday work schedule around, which means he'll be in town after all. Which is great! He's never missed a Christmas at home. But ummmmm he'll want to sleep in his bedroom, which means we'll be sharing a room after all. I'm so, so sorry.

GABE

It's cool. We'll look more like a couple that way anyway.

Unless you snore. Do you snore? Because I didn't sign up for that.

DARBY

Too late now.

One day before departure:

GABE

How do you feel about showing up in my shitty landscaping truck?

DARBY

I would absolutely love that.

GABE

It has no muffler and gets about six miles to the gallon.

DARBY

You had me at shitty truck.

GABE

So I was thinking that maybe part of bad boyfriending could be that I'm a tickler. I tickle everybody.

DARBY

Absolutely not.

GABE

Ugh, fine.

But you're required to sit on my lap anytime we're in the same room.

DARBY

Ugh, fine.

Is it weird that I'm kind of looking forward to this?

Oh God, I scared you off.

This is why all the guys I date run away from me, isn't it? I come on too strong.

Can you please send me Jonesy's number so I can ask him to be my fake boyfriend?

GABE

Don't you dare. I had to jump into a cold shower after you said yes to lap-sitting.

DARBY

Ha. See you tomorrow after work?

GABE

See you then. Sleep well.

DARBY

You too.

CHAPTER FOUR

Darby

I hear Gabe coming up my street before I see him. He wasn't kidding about that muffler.

Once he pulls into my driveway, I drag my suitcase and bag of wrapped gifts onto the porch and lock my front door, then turn to examine his truck.

"What do you think?" He hops out and ambles up my sidewalk, grabbing my bags before I can object.

"Wow. You didn't oversell it."

The body of the truck is a faded red, but the passenger side door is a bright, shiny blue, clearly a post-accident replacement that nobody bothered to paint match. The rest of the body isn't in bad shape if you don't mind some dings and scratches, but his front bumper is crumpled on the driver's side.

He's laughing as he opens the passenger side door and

settles my luggage in the back, then he pats the side panel fondly. "She and I have been through a lot together."

"She?"

"She's the main lady in my life. I bought her about five years ago when I got serious about landscaping. We've hauled a lot of mulch, Bessie and I. Someday soon I'll fix her up and make her shiny again." After one more pat, he offers me his hand, clearly planning to help me with the tall step up.

I hesitate before I slide my fingers into his. He's even better-looking than I remember from our meeting in the library, but that could be thanks to our countless texts and phone calls over the past month. I've gotten to know his humor, his quirks, even his daily routines. I expected to be perfectly comfortable in his company this week, but the physical reality of him is... different.

When he shifts his weight from foot to foot, I realize I've been making him wait while I overthought the mere act of touching him. I fight back a blush and grab his hand. It's warm and a little rough, and he easily boosts me onto the smoothly worn bench seat. The cab smells good, a little earthy and a little caffeinated. The latter scent is from the two take-out cups nestled into the holders, gently steaming in the December air.

"Coffee? At this hour?" We had to wait until I was off work to set out on our three-hour trip to Oak Brook, and it's fast approaching five p.m. "Planning to offer me cocaine next?"

He laughs as he lopes around the front and settles himself behind the wheel, firing up that bone marrow-rattling engine. "The traffic outside of Chicago's probably going to be crazy, so I thought we could use the pick-me-up."

We've barely buckled ourselves in before he's racing down the driveway and leaving my house in the rearview.

"Good thing I've got a cast-iron stomach," I say, glancing over at the man next to me and doing a double-take. "Gabe, is that a Cardinals shirt?"

He doesn't look away from the road, but his smile is wicked. "Sure is. Think your dad will hate it?"

My giddy delight almost chokes me. "It's *perfect*. He'll probably make you sleep outside."

His eyes slide over to mine, and we share a conspiratorial laugh. "Good. Because wearing this might actually give me a rash."

"Chicago fan?" Beaucoeur is equidistant between Chicago and St. Louis, so the Cubs/Cards fandom divide is real, and it's bitter.

"You know it." Then he taps the lid on one of the coffee cups. "I didn't know your order, so I got one with cream and sugar and left one black."

"Black, please." I reach for the one he indicates. "How do you take yours?"

"Same," he says.

"Oh!" I extend the cup to him. "I can take the other one. I don't mind."

He ignores me and plucks the other one from the holder. "No worries."

I watch as he sips from the milky, sweetened cup, feeling guilty that I ended up with the coffee style we both prefer.

"Thank you." I wrap my hands around the cup, grateful for the warmth. "This was really thoughtful."

"I won't let it happen again," he says. I look at him in confusion, and he winks. "Bad boyfriend only from here on out."

No other guy I know can get away with winking that way he does. I laugh and sip my coffee, strong and dark, just like I like it.

"So we both like black coffee," he says. "I almost grabbed you a sandwich too, but I didn't want to pick at random."

"Anything without meat is good. I'm a vegetarian," I tell him.

"No burgers. Noted. What else should we know about each other?"

He's smart to ask. In all of our pre-trip conversations, we didn't cover many of the boring details.

"I dunno," I say. "Middle name?"

"Yawn. We can do better than that." The setting sun hits us as we turn toward the highway that'll take us to the 'burbs. "Sunglasses?"

He gestures to his glove box, and I pop it open to discover a tidy stack of registration paperwork, a few note-books, the sunglasses, and nothing else.

"Okay, so you're organized," I say, handing them over. "What else? I'm talking basic bio, dating history, how we met, how long we've been together, that kind of thing."

He slips on the sunnies. "Let's see... I was born in Wiesbaden, Germany." He anticipates my question and answers without me needing to ask. "My dad's career Army. I was born on base. We moved around a lot and came to Beaucoeur as I was starting high school. My parents and younger brother moved my senior year when he was assigned to a new duty station, but I stayed behind."

He's glossing over the GED thing, but he didn't want to talk about it last time, so I don't pry. "Hobbies? Girl-friends? Bodies in your crawl space?"

"I like being outside and working with my hands. I like Marvel movies and *John Wick*. I don't spend much time in libraries."

"That's how it always is with you Wiesbaden boys," I say. "And don't think I didn't notice you didn't answer about the bodies."

He takes a long swallow of his coffee. "I have committed no murders, and I haven't seriously dated anybody in a long time."

"What's a long time?"

He takes a hand off the steering wheel to rub his jaw. He hasn't shaved, and his knuckles rasp along the stubble. "Not since shortly after I moved out on my own. So a couple of years."

I try to follow his vague timeline and don't like what I came up with. "Wait. Gabe, how old are you?"

"Twenty-six."

My brain stalls out over the math, and then I moan. "Oh my God, I'm bringing home a baby."

"How old are *you*?" The sun finally vanishes, so he pulls off his sunglasses and peers at me.

"Thirty-four!"

"Pssht. Eight years is nothing." He shrugs and turns back to the road, apparently unconcerned by my cradle-robbing.

"You were in kindergarten when I was getting boobs!"

"Awesome." He looks at me again, but this time his attention's on my chest. "Nice job with that, by the way."

When I squawk in outrage, he just laughs. "What's the big deal? Adults born in different decades can date. We both have jobs and bills and parents we've let down one way or another."

I'm still stuck on the 365-times-eight days separating us. "So when you were a high school senior, I was—"

"You were starting a career as a badass librarian. That's so hot."

His utter lack of concern is starting to calm me down. Maybe he's right. I mean, never once in all our conversations over the past month did I feel like I was talking to someone with a vast difference in life experiences.

I do a quick check-in with all my pertinent body parts. Brain says it's a little weird. Nose says he smells divine, no matter the age. Vagina has zero objections to any part of him. Heart asks to be excluded from this line of questioning.

Okay then. Guess we're carrying on.

"You all good over there?" He grins at me, and my vagina lets me know that its "zero objections" has turned into an "invite him in." This is getting out of control.

"Yeah, all good." I squeeze my thighs together and think about the Dewey Decimal System.

"Your turn. Hit me with your deets."

Oh boy. Here we go, world's most boring origin story. "So I grew up in Oak Brook. My dad's an insurance agent, and my mom stayed home with us. She's an amazing quilter and spends lots of her time on that."

"Who's us?"

"Older sister, younger brother. Me in the middle."

"Got it."

He really doesn't, but he'll find out soon enough.

"My sister married her college sweetheart, and they have four loud children. My brother's the world's most immature commercial airline pilot who never gets flack at family dinners for being single. That honor's reserved for me."

"The patriarchy hurts us all." He shakes his head. "So how'd you end up in Beaucoeur?"

"I got a scholarship to Rayman College and almost immediately switched from pre-med to library science." I was elated to discover how orderly it is, putting everything in its place. "After graduation, I lucked into a job at the Beaucoeur Library and just... stayed."

I glance over at him, still a little intimidated to be bringing this hot younger man home with me. He's all active and outdoorsy, while I'm a stay-inside-reading type. I expect him to be totally bored by me within an hour.

We both fall silent for a bit, and then he asks, "So why don't you have a boyfriend?"

Embarrassed heat crawls up my neck. "Why don't you have a girlfriend?"

No embarrassment from him. "Because I needed to spend the past few years figuring out how to be an adult, and that didn't leave a lot of room for me to be a decent partner for anybody else."

"Hmm. I wish the guys I've dated had been that mature." Just like I wish I'd been mature enough to tell them what I needed rather than swallowing my frustrations until the relationships imploded. I turn my head and watch the farmland whiz by my window, fields full of yellowing chaff left behind after the harvest.

"So how do you know Faith?" he asks, presumably as eager to get away from this topic as I am.

"She uses the library conference rooms for some of her community presentations. We've gotten friendly over the years."

Faith Fox runs an educational non-profit that provides services like tutoring and adult literacy. "I take it you know her from the... the GED thing?"

I hesitate over the question, not wanting him to clam up the way he did during our first meeting, but he just nods. Maybe our texting helped ease him into sharing. His body language is relaxed, and he swirls his coffee before speaking.

"Yeah. After my family moved, it was... not a fun time." His jaw clenches. "It was a lot harder to support myself than I realized. I ended up dropping out with a couple of months to go in the school year, but there was no way I was going to tell my dad he was right. So I made it work here."

"That's a lot for an eighteen-year-old."

He shrugs. "Did what I had to do. It turns out getting a business up and running's easier with a degree, and, well, that's where Faith comes in."

"She's good like that." Time to let him off the hook; I'd imagine talking about that isn't fun for him. "So maybe that's our story. Our mutual friend introduced us a few months ago, and we've been seeing each other since then. Your family's out of town, so you're doing Christmas with me."

"Christmas with my best girl," he says easily, and for a second I let myself imagine that he actually means it.

CHAPTER FIVE

Gabe

Talking to Darby is fun.

It's such a basic thought to float through my head as we take the exit off the interstate for her parents' home, but it's true. We talked the whole trip, so much so that my voice is hoarse, and I'm feeling grateful that I met her now and not a couple of years ago, when I was drinking too much and not taking anything seriously.

Then I remember why I'm here, and I clench my hands around the steering wheel as we wait for the light at a busy intersection near a Cheesecake Factory attached to a shopping mall. This is all a joke, something I'm doing because I was bored and a little lonely, and it amused me. If things go according to plan, her family will be ecstatic to never see me again after this week. But it only took a few minutes into our first meeting to figure out that I liked this woman. The text messages made my infatuation grow, and the car ride just hammered it home. Part of me wishes I was going to meet her parents for real, and not while wearing Cardinals gear I bought for the occasion.

Oh well. It'll make for a good story someday.

By now, we've pulled up outside a brick house that looks like Macaulay Culkin's from *Home Alone*. Christmas lights outline the roof, and wreaths hang in every window. Somehow you just know there's good eggnog waiting for you inside.

I turn the truck off, silently apologizing to everybody in this nice neighborhood that I didn't pick Darby up in my Charger this afternoon.

"I don't think I can do this."

She says the words quietly, directing them at her hands, clenched into balls in her lap.

"What do you mean?"

She falls back against the seat, gesturing to the house. "The fake boyfriend thing, asking you to be a terrible person, lying to my family for days. I can't pull that off. That's not what I do."

She exhales, deflating a little, and I unbuckle my seat belt to face her. I've known her for a month, but it's clear that lying and sabotage don't come easily to her.

Good thing she's got me.

"Okay, hear me out, and know that no matter what, I'll do whatever you think is best." She turns too, her forehead knotted with worry. "Is what you've been doing working for you?"

Her expression's clouded, so I try to make her see what I see when I look at her.

"You're a cool girl who loves her job and her friends. But your family makes you so miserable that you're bringing home a stranger to get them off your back. Maybe what you've been doing isn't working."

She nibbles on that delectable lower lip but doesn't respond. Since she's not disagreeing with me, I continue. "People stick up for themselves in all kinds of ways. When I was a teenager, I thought I was doing that by arguing nonstop with my dad. And your approach up until today has been..."

She hears the question in my voice. "Avoidance."

Ah, avoidance. Not something I've ever personally understood. But if that's her MO, no wonder she's getting cold feet.

"So this time you're not choosing avoidance. What would you say you're hoping to do this week?"

"Be passive-aggressive," she says. "Wait, be *aggressive*-aggressive."

"You're being creative," I correct her. "You're trying a new approach to a problem you haven't been able to solve. What's the worst that can happen?"

"My parents kick us out and never speak to me again?"

"I highly doubt that. Even my parents talk to me after I was an insufferable shit for all those years."

She studies my face, her eyes reflecting the ambient light in the dark truck cab. "Yeah, why aren't you with them this year? I'll be honest, I kind of assumed there was bad blood between you."

A car heads down the street in our direction, the driver staring hard at the crumpled fender illuminated by his headlights as he cruises past. I glare back before returning my attention to Darby.

"Thankfully, no. We're all good now. But my brother and his wife just had a baby, so Mom and Dad flew to

Hawaii. That's where he's stationed, and me going along was one person too many to cram into military housing for a week."

Darby latches on to the most important part of my explanation.

"Your brother's military?"

"Yep. I'm the disappointment of the family."

I keep my tone light, but I'm afraid she hears what I'm not saying. I don't fit in with my Army dad and my Army brother, and even though I've gotten my life together, there's no reason for me to fly all the way to Hawaii to feel out of place.

Her hand darts out to cover mine, and she squeezes. I'm so grateful for that comforting touch that for a second I let myself pretend this is real. I've just spent a fun few hours with an amazing woman, and now I'm going to meet her parents as my best self. But that's not what's happening here, is it?

My eyes slide over her shoulder to her house, where the curtain in the front window twitches. Wondering what kind of scrap vehicle is messing with their property values, no doubt.

"So how do you wanna play this?" I ask. "Do you want me to be the perfect boyfriend or the boyfriend from hell? Or do you want me to turn around and drive home?"

She turns her head and now we're both studying the house, with its huge wreath on the glossy black front door and its garland-wrapped light post. It screams Christmas, as does Darby in her red fleece and pompom-topped hat. She'd look right at home in a Norman Rockwell painting.

Her wicked smile isn't Rockwell-ish, though.

"You know what? Let's do it. Bad boyfriend activate. I

never want to hear them ask me a single thing about my love life ever again after this week."

Disappointment whispers through my chest. Part of me wanted her to call it all off, tell me I wouldn't have to put all my nefarious plans into action. But I'm here to help Darby, and if she still wants to go through with it, I'll play my part.

"Okay, then the fake bad boyfriending starts now. But you have to tell me if I ever make you uncomfortable, and I'll stop immediately."

Her green-brown eyes soften. "That's nice of you. So a safe word, then?"

Smart. She's so damn smart. I glance down the street, lined with expensive homes. Every last one has tastefully boring landscaping and casually elegant holiday decorations. I'd feel out of place even if I wasn't going out of my way to ruin these people's Christmas.

Inspiration strikes. "Is 'Grinch' too on the nose?"

She gives a silvery peal of laughter. "It's perfect. But don't expect to hear it. It's going to take a miracle to get my family to back off."

She bites her lip again and looks back at the house where she grew up. "My therapist tells me I need to get better about setting boundaries and letting people know when they've crossed a line." She lifts her shoulders and lets them fall. "So I guess it's kind of my fault that they don't know how much their little jokes hurt my feelings over the years."

"Don't blame yourself. And don't worry; Bad Gabe is here to be your weapon. You can nuke them from space." She laughs, as I hoped she would. "If they do kick us out, we'll just drive back to my place, watch *The Long Kiss Goodnight*, and eat our weight in pork buns."

"What's *The Long Kiss Goodnight*?"

I gasp in mock horror. "It's only the best Christmas action movie."

"Better than *Die Hard*?" Her voice is skeptical.

"By a mile."

"Wow. Okay. Always good to have a backup plan." She still sounds a little nervous, but before she opens the door and lets the outside world in, I put my hand on her knee. She stills, her eyes flying to mine, and I swallow hard before I speak.

"I need you to know something. If you really were my girlfriend, I'd jump out of this truck and open your door for you and help you down." I hold her gaze as I talk, and my thumb makes a little circle on her jeans. "I'd carry your bags in and put them anywhere in that house you want. And I'd be so damn polite to your parents, they'd get bored within five minutes." I'd also kiss her the minute I got her alone in the room we'd be sharing, but she doesn't need to know that part.

She might be thinking something similar because a shiver runs through her body. I know because my fingers are still resting on her leg. Oops.

"Bad Gabe doesn't do any of that though," she says, and I strain to hear if there's disappointment in her voice.

"No," I agree. "He doesn't."

Then she blows out a breath and throws her shoulders back. "No worries. I packed that suitcase. I can carry it."

"I still don't like it," I grumble, popping open my door. It lets the cold evening air rush in, destroying the cozy cocoon we've created for ourselves. I step outside and reach behind the driver's seat to grab my duffel.

"If things go right, you can be as happily unattached as you want to be for the rest of your life," I tell her.

"Yeah," she says, not quite meeting my eyes over the interior of the truck. "Yay."

Then I turn and walk toward this houseful of strangers whose Christmas I'm about to make really weird.

CHAPTER SIX

Darby

I don't quite know how to explain it, but I can see the moment Gabe turns himself into Bad Gabe. He slings his bag over his shoulder, and the playfulness drains from his face. One corner of his mouth twists up, and he runs his eyes down my body with a cocky smirk.

"You ready to get this over with, babe?" He jerks his head toward the house, then starts up the big curved sidewalk leading to the front door.

I'm too stunned to move for a second. God, even his voice is different. Smug and a little bored, like he's agreed to do something he has zero interest in, and he's going to hold it over my head forever.

But I've got a part to play too, so I yank my suitcase out of the back, struggling a little when the wheel gets tangled in the seat belt. Once it pops free, I stagger backward, then grab the bag of gifts and slam the door shut, trotting up the sidewalk after him.

"Get it over with? I thought you wanted to meet my family."

He glances over his shoulder. "Of course I do, babe." He whips back around and saunters to the front stoop, impatiently tapping his foot while he waits for me to join him.

Oh God, is my family watching this? I'm sure I look stressed because I'm *feeling* stressed, dammit. He's way better at this than I expected.

I finally join him, the chill seeping into my skin as my suitcase bounces up the concrete steps behind me, slamming into my calves. My hand's on the doorknob when I realize there's something important we haven't covered.

"Kissing!" I hiss.

He looks startled, and his gaze snaps to the top of the doorframe. "Oh God, are your parents mistletoe people?"

"No! I mean, should we be kissing?" I can't believe that in all those weeks of calls and texts, we never thought to discuss it. "And holding hands? Hugging? People in relationships do that, right?"

My mind flashes back to Gabe not shaking my hand at our first meeting and then to his featherlight touch on my knee in the cab of his truck. I suppress a shiver; no contact is far safer for my peace of mind. But who brings a boyfriend home for Christmas and maintains a polite distance?

"Hey. It's okay." He spins me to face him, resting his hands on my shoulders. "We'll just—"

Before he can finish that thought, the door flies open to reveal my mom. "Honey! Welcome home! Come inside. It's freezing out."

Gabe drops his hands, the warmth draining from his face, and steps through the door with his bag over his shoulder. I trail behind him, humping my suitcase over the doorjamb.

"Hi, Mom."

She wraps her arms around me and folds me into a Mom hug. You know the kind: soft, comfortable, warm, a little too clingy, but you wouldn't have it any other way. Yet again I'm hit with doubts about what I'm doing here. This is way too dramatic. I'm the child who doesn't complain or make demands. I definitely don't run elaborate schemes designed to fool my whole family. The temptation to shout "Grinch!" surges, but I choke it back.

My mom releases me and turns to my alleged boyfriend. "Hello, Gabe. I'm Margaret. Let me look at you." She reaches up to cup his cheeks. *This is not a drill. She is resting her hands on his cheeks.* "Do you know how much I've worried about my little Darby ending up all alone? And now she's brought home such a handsome young man."

I absolutely want to die. Thank God this isn't real; an actual boyfriend would probably run screaming. But now the question is, what's Gabe going to do? His expression is unreadable, not Good Gabe, but not Bad Gabe either. For a split second, I see the Good Gabe smile peek through. He's amused. He thinks her concern over me is cute. He's going to crack and ruin everything—or maybe save everything.

Then he pulls out that one-sided smirk I'm starting to recognize as Bad Gabe's calling card. He huffs a little laugh and glances over at me. "Wow, babe. If I'd known you were so hard up, I wouldn't have tried so hard on our first date. You could've paid for your own drinks."

It's an appalling thing to say, which of course makes it perfect. My mother yanks her hands away, taking a step back and cutting her eyes toward me.

"He's just kidding," I say with a brittle laugh. "Aren't you?"

He sucks in his cheeks before answering. "Sure. Kidding. So where are we sleeping?" He looks toward the stairs.

"Darby's room," my mom says. "Third door on the left."

He nods and heads for the second floor, not waiting for me. But before he hits the second step, he calls over his shoulder, "I'm starving, babe. Think you could find me a sandwich?"

Then he continues climbing the stairs, and I notice something sticking out from the hem of his jeans and getting caught under his work boot.

"Hold up," I call. "What's that?"

I trot up to him and bend down to tug it loose. When I do, I end up holding the sleaziest black-and-purple thong I've ever seen.

"Oh shit. Sorry, babe." He snatches it from my hand and crams it into his pocket. "Must've gotten mixed up in the laundry."

That evil, evil genius. I'm desperately biting back a giggle as I slam my hands on my hips. "Those aren't mine, Gabriel."

He holds up his hands apologetically, although his face is the farthest thing from apologetic. "Guess I need to purge my collection. Anyway, sandwich?" Then he takes the stairs two at a time, leaving me to deal with my stunned mother.

"Well... he was... I wasn't..."

She's staring at the landing where he's disappeared, and my first instinct is to trip all over myself to make excuses for him. But you know what? No. An actual boyfriend would've been freaked out by that little speech about her sad single daughter.

If you don't communicate your boundaries, how will anyone know when they've crossed them? I've never been good at putting that therapy mantra into practice, but if not now, when? If not me, who? If not directed at my mother, what am I even doing here this week?

"You made me sound pathetic just now, Mom."

She blinks a few times, likely surprised to get the tiniest bit of pushback from me. "Oh honey, I'm sorry. I didn't mean it like that."

"It's fine," I say quickly. Now that it's out of her system she'll probably calm down, so there's no need to upset her. I hug her again, resting my head on her shoulder. Her hair, more gray than brown now, tangles with my earring as she squeezes me back.

"We're just so excited you brought someone home with you. We only want you to be happy, but with every year that goes by..." She releases me, and her eyes drift upstairs again. I'm pretty sure we're both thinking about that damn thong. "Was he serious about the sandwich?"

Good question. "I'm not sure. Why don't I head up and check?"

I haul my suitcase—I have literally never thought about my luggage as much as I have in the past five minutes—up the stairs and ease my door open to find Gabe leaning awkwardly against the wall farthest from the bed. He's staring at the pink-and-white quilt covering it. Mom made it for me when I turned thirteen, and it still makes me smile.

"It doesn't bite," I tell him as I shut the door behind me. "It's a mattress, not a torture device."

"Ha. How'd it go?"

I climb onto the bed and kick off my shoes.

"You were perfect, and by that I mean perfectly awful."

He shrugs modestly. "I told you, I have a history of terrible behavior to draw from."

"Your poor ex-girlfriends." A horrifying thought strikes me. "Wait, is that where you got that thong?"

"God, no. I bought a new one just for this."

"What a gentleman."

He wanders to the window, pulling back the curtain to peer out into the backyard. "Using old underwear would be beyond tacky." He turns and grins at me. Good Gabe in the house.

"Definitely," I say as he steps away from the window and resumes his position by the wall. "Okay, what's going on here?"

He swallows hard, his throat working. "It's so small."

"It's a queen." I pat the ample space next to me. "That's not small."

He still looks dubious. "I'll just sleep on the floor."

I snort and flop backward onto the bed, flinging my arms and legs out like a starfish.

"See? Still plenty of room. We'd barely touch."

"The floor's no big deal," he insists. "I slept on a futon for a full year. A carpeted floor is nothing."

I sit up. "Sure, but you were sleeping on that futon when you were, what, nineteen and made of rubber?"

"Try twenty-five. My body's impervious to pain."

I wince. "Wow. You do own sheets and towels now, right? Because if not, I'll ask Santa to bring you some."

He just laughs and folds his arm over his chest. "I wasn't kidding about that sandwich, *babe*. My manly hunger needs to be met."

I sigh and haul myself upright. "Okay. Guess it's time for round two. Shall we?"

A light sparks in his eyes. "I've got a better idea. I'm pretty sure I've got a headache after driving you here, and I can't possibly spend any time with your parents tonight. Want to bring me dinner on a tray?"

"Absolutely," I say slowly. And I prove that he's not the only evil genius among us. "But only if you text me constantly with requests that have me running up and down all night. Maybe send the sandwich back a few times until it's perfect."

He barks a laugh. "Love it. I'm very picky. Sandwich *squares*, not triangles. And I better not see any crust."

He holds up his hand for a high five, which I return. It's possibly the most platonic thing that's ever happened in this room—and I was a virgin until I was nineteen. Speaking of.

"Hey, about the kissing thing."

He smiles lazily. "Still thinking about it, huh?"

"No!" Yes. Very much. "What should we do around my family?"

He makes a beeline for his favorite spot against the wall before answering.

"Let's not overthink it. We should be comfortable with casual touches, but full-on making out in the public areas of the house probably won't be necessary."

"Probably?"

That wolfish grin again. "Probably. We'll play it by ear."

I'm suddenly having trouble drawing air into my

lungs, so I squeak my agreement and dart out of the room. After a few seconds to get my breathing under control, I head downstairs for an evening of waiting on my boyfriend hand and foot while my parents wonder if I've lost my mind.

Gotta love it when a plan comes together.

CHAPTER SEVEN

Gabe

We stay in Darby's room as late as possible the next morning, sending our favorite TikToks back and forth and hoping her parents will make all kinds of wrong assumptions about what we're really getting up to behind her closed door. It's hunger that finally sends us downstairs.

In the kitchen, I get my first glimpse of Darby's father. He and Margaret are a perfect pair, both comfortably plump and full of smiles and Midwestern Christmas cheer. Since I grew up in a rigid military household, I don't really know what to expect at the St. Claires'. What I find is a spacious kitchen that's full of sunlight and cozily cluttered with mail, cookbooks, potted plants, and take-out fliers. Darby's mom is wearing a plain red apron as she pulls a tray of cookies out of the oven, and her dad's sitting on a stool at the marble island, sipping from a mug with a madly grinning gingerbread man printed on the side.

"Sugar plum!" he calls when we walk into the room, standing up and folding Darby into a hug. The St. Claires are huggers.

"Hi, Daddy." She rests her cheek on his chest. "Does your Christmas vacation start now?"

"You've got me twenty-four seven for the duration." Then he turns to me, his expression hardening. "You must be Darby's friend. I'm Clint."

He reaches out to shake my hand, and the squeeze is a bit harder than I'm expecting. His wife must've given him an earful about me already.

"I'm her *boy*friend. Gabe." I hit the *boy* part hard, knowing that the ownership thing matters to some men and might creep out her father.

"Sorry I wasn't home when you kids got in. I stayed late finishing end-of-year paperwork at the office." He folds his arms over his chest and glares icicles at me. "Sounds like you kept Darby on her toes though."

Margaret's laugh is forced as she diverts the conversation. "What can I get you kids for breakfast? Or early lunch, I should say."

Before Darby can answer, I jump in with, "Got any beer?"

Clint pointedly looks at the clock on the oven, which reads 10:18 a.m., but he crosses to the fridge and pulls out an IPA with a label I don't recognize. After a moment, he sets his coffee down and pulls out a second one for himself. "It's a holiday, after all." He hands me a bottle and clinks the necks together before taking a long pull of his.

"Thanks," I say, taking a sip. I didn't really want one, and now I'm stuck nursing it.

Darby rubs my back. "What sounds good? Mom does a mean grilled cheese."

I forget about Bad Gabe for a second. "Yeah? I love a grilled cheese." I grin at Margaret, who smiles back. Shit. Bad boyfriend. Be bad. "But no crusts."

Her smile flattens. "Yes. I remember from last night."

She heads to the fridge and starts pulling out sandwich fixings while I slouch back down, channeling sulky boredom as best as I can. But damn, this IPA is really good. I lift the label to check it out, and Clint raises his in salute.

"Moody Tongue. Made in Chicago."

"Dad loves it," Darby says. "Maybe we could hit the brewery sometime."

She swipes my bottle from me to steal a drink before handing it back. I almost fumble it when she chases a stray drop at the corner of her mouth with her tongue.

"I'd love that," I manage, raising the bottle to my lips so they're pressed where hers were moments ago. I haven't known a moment of peace since she brought up the question of kissing yesterday, but given how freaked out she looked about the whole thing, this secondhand contact might be the closest I get while we're here.

"That's quite a truck," Clint says. His tone is friendly, but it's clear to everyone in the kitchen that he hates it. It definitely makes me stop thinking about his daughter's mouth.

"Thanks." I take another sip. "Someday I'll restore it properly. It's a '95 Ford F-Series."

Interest sparks in his eyes. "Is it? A '95 you say?"

"Oh boy, here we go," Margaret mutters, and she and Darby both roll their eyes.

Darby senses my confusion and explains, "Dad loves classic cars, especially the newer classics. You're going to have to let him poke around under the hood now."

Clint shrugs his agreement. "I didn't recognize the body shape what with the..."

I grimace. "Yeah, the mismatched door's the first thing anybody really sees." I pat my pockets and pull out the keys. "Shall we?"

Before we leave the kitchen, Margaret calls, "Lunch in twenty!"

Clint ushers me out the front door, and the brittle brown grass crunches our feet as we head to the curb. He gives a low whistle. "I'll be damned."

I pat the hood. "I use her for work, but she's in no worse condition than the day I got her."

He circles the truck body, peeking into the back. "What is it that you do?"

Can you provide for my daughter, in other words. Darby's words came back to me: *My mother will hate that.* But what about her father?

"I'm a landscaper. I'm opening my own business next year, and part of the branding will be a complete overhaul." I run my thumb over one of the dings in her side panel. "I want her to be a good ad for the business, logo and all."

"Smart. May I?" He gestures at the hood, and I open the cab and pull the release. Once it's up, we contemplate her innards in silence. Clint eyeballs the fluid levels and taps the dipstick with his finger, although he stops short of pulling it out to check it. It's such a dad move that I have to smile.

"Got someone for insurance? Business, I mean." He's bent all the way over the engine now, poking at my spark plugs and jiggling some wires. I hope I'll be able to drive it home.

"I was planning to talk to my home and auto guy." I hesitate because this isn't what Darby would want, but I ask it anyway. "Darby says you're in insurance. Do you recommend anyone in Beaucoeur?"

His head pops out from under the hood like a ground-hog. "I can give you a couple of names. And I can also tell you a few of the questions you'll want to be asking to see if they're what you're looking for. If you want the advice, that is." He crosses his arms and waits.

This is a test, and even though I'm supposed to fail it —tell him to go to hell, tell him I make my own way—I actually want his advice.

Fuck it. I'll double up on shitty behavior at dinner tonight. Right now, I want this man's thoughts on starting a business.

"I do, if you're willing to share."

"Anything for my baby girl," he says. Then he unleashes a torrent of "be sure to ask this" and "you're going to want to do that" suggestions that have me scrambling for one of the glove box notebooks that I take with me to job sites.

As we head inside for lunch, he promises to get me in touch with one of his trusted guys in the Beaucoeur area, and we're exchanging phone numbers when we walk into the kitchen to wash the car grime off our hands.

While her dad's at the sink, Darby shoots me a *What the hell, man?* look, and I shrug apologetically. Mission failure. I'll do better starting now.

"Perfect timing," Margaret chirps after I trade places

with Clint, scrubbing the grease off my hands with candy cane-scented soap. She sets a platter of sandwiches in the middle of the island alongside a bowl of pasta salad. The scent of hot butter and toasty cheese makes me salivate. And Margaret actually did slice the crusts off of half the sandwiches. I'm oddly touched.

"This looks incredible," Darby says as we all grab plates and dig in. The kitchen is quiet while everybody chews. After a beat I nudge her, determined to get our plan back on track.

"Guess you didn't get your cooking skills from your mom." I have no idea if she can cook or not, but it feels like an appropriately dickish thing to say.

Unfortunately, it works a little too well, and Clint throws his head back in laughter.

"That's what I always tell her. She's never going to keep a man if she doesn't up her cooking game. Roast him a chicken! Bake lemon bars! Best way to a man's heart is through his stomach."

Darby slouches over her plate, her expression souring. "It's not the 1960s anymore. Men can cook too. Women also have full-time jobs, you know."

Oh hell. The instinct to defend Darby swells, but I've got ground to make up. I sling a possessive arm around her neck and pull her against my side.

"Just do what you can to keep me satisfied, and maybe I'll keep you around into the new year."

Her body's rigid, so I release her quickly, vowing to apologize to her later for bringing it up. But it does create an awkward break in the conversation that has her dad taking his empty plate to the sink and her mom hopping up to clean off the stovetop. With them both occupied, I lean closer to her and whisper, "I actually do a mean lasagna. Let me make it for you sometime."

She pulls away in surprise, and honestly I'm a little unsure of where that came from myself. We haven't talked about any post-Christmas plans. Presumably she goes on with her life and I go on with mine.

As I'm starting to imagine ways to keep Darby around after this week, a pleased little smile spreads across her face. "Did you hear that, Mom and Dad? Gabe just offered to make dinner for everyone tomorrow."

CHAPTER EIGHT

Darby

"Things could be going better."

We're in my bedroom changing into our pajamas after dinner—a dinner where Gabe mostly communicated in monosyllabic grunts, as he'd been doing all afternoon—and I feel like a coach offering post-game analysis.

"Yeah, I'll try harder," he says.

Dinner wasn't pleasant, but it wasn't really the disaster I clearly need to get my parents to stop nitpicking my dating prospects. We've got to up our game because right now, my dad's in danger of offering to drive to Beaucoeur next weekend to help Gabe buff out the dings on his magical truck.

"When's your brother get here?" he asks. "Maybe I could challenge him to a fight."

"What, like a physical brawl?"

Our backs are to each other while we change, and I resist the urge to look over my shoulder. The close quarters are tough enough without sneaking a peek, but the whisper of clothes going on and off his body is driving me nuts. And knowing that if I just turned around...

"A brawl on the St. Claire front lawn," he says thoughtfully, pulling me away from my lust-filled thoughts. "It'll be a Christmas the neighbors'll never forget."

"Absolutely not. Grinch Grinch Grinchy Grinch to that."

"Fine," he says. "You decent?"

"Yep." I turn to face him, and I snort when I see the redbirds all over his lounge pants. "Wait, are you secretly a Cardinals fan?"

"Hell no. But I'm dressing for the job I want."

He grins at me, and my breath catches in my throat. Gabe with a lazy smile is even sweeter than Mom's snickerdoodles. I blink a few times, needing to collect my wits before I can reply.

"The job you want is to be my dad's number one enemy?"

"If that's what it takes." He holds his hand out. "Shall we?"

I slip my fingers through his, enjoying the warmth of his palm a little too much, and we head downstairs to the TV room, where my parents are in their his-and-hers recliners, waiting on us to fire up a movie. My mom's got some quilt squares on her lap, and my dad sighs loudly when he realizes Gabe's dressed head-to-toe in Cardinals wear again.

"Good thing baseball's not in season," he mutters, and Gabe quirks a brow as we settle onto the couch.

"With some of the Cubs' trades recently? Yeah, I can see why you'd want to put off playing actual games."

"Boys!" My mom shuts down the debate. "We are here to watch the snowiest Hallmark Christmas movie we can find. There will be no sports talk in this holiday space."

Like every room in the house this time of year, the den is a cozy winter wonderland, from the twinkling lights on the Christmas tree to the array of porcelain reindeer prancing across the mantle where a fire burns merrily away.

"The decorations look great this year, Mom."

I drift over to the built-in bookshelves and swap a couple of the book club fiction titles so they're alphabetical on the shelf.

"Thanks, sweetie. There's eggnog in the fridge and hot chocolate on the stove."

"Mom makes the best hot chocolate," I tell Gabe. "Want some?"

"I guess," he says, sounding annoyed at the idea of a hot seasonal drink poured just for him. As I head into the kitchen, he snaps his fingers and gives a sharp whistle. I pause in the doorway, both impressed and appalled that he just summoned me like a dog.

"Babe," he says, "make sure it's not *too* hot. You know the roof of my mouth is sensitive."

When both of my parents turn to me with identical "is he for real?" expressions, Gabe looks over their heads and mouths a laughing apology. As far as bad boyfriend demands go, it's the goofiest one yet, and I hustle out of the room so nobody catches me giggling over it.

When I return, I hand Gabe one of the snowman

mugs from my Mom's limitless supply. "Don't worry, I blew on it for you."

He grunts his thanks, but as he goes to sip, his eyes meet mine, and they're dancing with suppressed mirth. "You can blow on something else later," he whispers just loudly enough for my parents to hear.

My cheeks flame even though I know it's all an act. My dad doesn't, though, and gruffly clears his throat. "Enough chatter. What are we watching?"

Mom grabs the remote and starts scrolling through the films she's been saving to the DVR all month long. "Let's see... we've got one about a Christmas cookie bake-off, one where they're snowed in at a bed and breakfast. Oh, this one's got the girl pretending that the man's her boyfriend for the big company Christmas party!"

"Not that one," I blurt. Gabe's body quakes with silent laughter, and I elbow him. "How about the B&B blizzard?"

"Good choice," Dad says, and Mom and I exchange smiles. No matter what we choose, he'll be asleep in his chair within twenty minutes.

Just before she presses play, Gabe takes another sip of hot chocolate and gags. "Eww, babe, can you add some alcohol to this? I don't care what, just something to take the edge off the taste."

For a beat, the only sound in the living room is a log popping in the fireplace. Mom takes her hot chocolate recipe seriously, and this is a direct challenge to her skills.

"Um, sure," I say. "Be right back."

Nobody talks the whole time I'm gone, and I hastily select the bottle of Bailey's in my parents' liquor cabinet. I have no idea what Gabe's drink of choice is, so I pick what I'd want in my own hot chocolate and hustle back.

"Finally ready?" Mom's voice sounds a little strained as I settle onto the couch next to Gabe, acutely aware of his body pressing against mine.

"Ready!" I chirp, as if my boyfriend making childish demands that he expects me to satisfy is a totally normal thing.

She hits play, and just as we suspected, my dad's snoring shortly after the opening credits, leaving Mom and me to playfully roast the dialogue the beret-clad heroine's spouting while Gabe plays on his phone and ignores us. He eventually pulls up a YouTube video showing proper weight-lifting technique, and my mom sends me an incredulous glance when the sound of manly grunts and clinking metal plates starts to compete with the dialogue onscreen.

"Hey." I nudge Gabe. "Mind putting that away?"

He sighs theatrically, but he pockets his phone. "Fiiiine. I was just watching a video Jonesy sent." He crosses his arm and glares at the TV. "Who's that guy?"

"That's the hero," says my eternally patient mom.

"Why's he so upset?"

"There's. A. Blizzard."

I bite my lip. Even the queen of calm is getting irritated. Excellent.

"These movies have blizzards all the time. It's like all Hallmark people live in a snow globe," Gabe says.

"That's why we love them!" My mom says before frowning. "But I don't know why this hero didn't think to check the weather reports."

"Especially since he's headed to a remote cabin where he could get snowed in," I agree.

We watch in silence for a bit as the hero stomps his

way through the tiny regional airport, insulting the hero-ine's hometown.

"I just don't understand why they couldn't find a handsomer man to cast in this," Gabe says, and I laugh at my mother's outraged gasp.

"What? He's perfectly lovely!" she declares.

Gabe leans forward to peer at the TV, making a show of studying the character grumpily checking into the B&B after his flight was canceled due to snow. "Nah. No way to women want a weak-chinned man with an obvious hairpiece."

My mom blinks. "That's not a hairpiece. Is it?" She pauses the film on a close-up shot of the hero's thick mane of sandy-blond hair.

"See there?" Gabe stands and walks to the TV, pointing at the hero's hairline. "It's too straight across his forehead."

She sets aside her sewing and stands to joins him, her nose almost brushing the glass as she leans close. "Well, I'll be. I think you're right!"

"I'm always right." He ambles back to the couch but settles himself on the floor in front of me. "Back rub, babe?" He tilts his head back to look up at me, a boyish smile on his face, and I can't help but grin back.

"Sure, you moocher." I set my mug down and rest my hands on his shoulders, digging my thumbs into his muscles.

Gabe Dickenson has *so many muscles.*

He hums gratefully as I work, and I move from his neck down to his shoulders, marveling in the strength I'm encountering with every sweep of my hands. Land-scaping must be a hell of a workout. When I reach his back, he twists away. "Hang on." Then my heart stutters to a halt when he reaches behind him to grab the back of his long-sleeved T-shirt, pulling it over his head.

"Oh, ummm..." I can't seem to find any words, not with Gabe's bare back on display in front of me. Between the TV, the fireplace, and the Christmas tree lights, there's enough illumination to see the many dips and swells of his muscles, along with the long curve of his spine.

I tentatively rest my hands on his skin, and he makes a noise deep in his throat that has my mother glancing over at us.

"Oh! Oh." She stands abruptly. "I'll just... run to the bathroom."

She pauses the film and darts out of the room, leaving us alone with my sleeping father.

I lean forward to whisper, "This is the weirdest family movie night of my life."

"Honestly, same." He twists around, bringing his lips close to my ear. "How would your mom feel about walking back in here to find us making out?"

His breath tickles my cheek, and I shiver. Every time we've touched today, my body's reacted.

"She'd be freaked," I whisper back. Hell, I'd be freaked. Why hadn't Faith sent me a less attractive fake boyfriend?

"Then I guess we'd better do it." He glides onto the couch in one sinuous movement, taking my hand in his. And just like that, I'm so damn grateful Faith sent me such an attractive fake boyfriend.

"I guess so," I say as my soul leaves my body to hover near the ceiling where it won't miss a second of whatever's about to happen to the rest of me. "This is playing it by ear, right?"

With no idea what to expect, I close my eyes and lift my face in his direction, waiting for the press of his lips. Instead, I hear an amused chuckle.

"You're so damn cute." He slides a hand behind my head, and when he grips my neck, my eyes pop open. He's Good Gabe again, his expression gentle. But when his mouth descends on mine, there's nothing gentle about his kiss. He's insistent, sweeping his tongue along the seam of my lips and nibbling on the corner of my mouth until I open for him. His hand moves to my hair and tightens, while his other hand slides along my shoulder to rest at the base of my throat, his thumb finding the hollow where my pulse flutters wildly.

The fireplace isn't the only thing blazing once his tongue meets mine. I wrap my arms around his neck and kiss him back, not sure if this is for my family's sake or for my own. I'm just working up the courage to move onto his lap when my mom's voice drifts from the kitchen.

"Oh, look! It's snowing!"

CHAPTER NINE

Gabe

Am I worked up? Absolutely. Do I want to hear Darby's father snorting himself awake while I'm trying to deal with a hard-on? Absolutely not.

"Whazzat?" Clint says groggily as Darby scrambles upright, leaving me cold and shirtless in her family's living room.

"It's snowing!" Margaret says again from the kitchen, and Clint makes the patented dad creaks and grunts as he pulls himself to his feet.

"You kids want to—" He glances our way, blanches, and immediately turns on his heel, muttering all the way out of the room. After he's gone, Darby collapses into giggles, falling forward against my chest. I can't resist wrapping my arms around her and holding her close, pressing her warm curves against me.

This is not helpful for my very alert dick.

"Think they're regretting my choice of men yet?" she whispers.

"Doing my best," I say as she pushes away from me. "Did you want to go look at the snow?"

She nods a little sheepishly. "I do. It's the first one of the year."

"And chicks dig that. I get it, *babe*." I hit the last word hard, hoping it'll make her laugh. It does, and warmth fills my chest, a different kind of warmth from the one I was feeling in my pants moments ago. The sensation is... nice. Unexpected, but nice.

Shit.

Feeling suddenly vulnerable, I reach for my shirt on the floor, but Darby puts her hand on my knee. "Wait a second."

I freeze as her eyes roam over my wrist and up my arm.

"A tree. I wondered."

She doesn't touch the black lines that make up the roots, trunk, and branches of my tattoo, although I wish she would.

"It's a birch." I don't know why I'm speaking so quietly. The design isn't a secret, necessarily, but I haven't actually explained it to anyone else and I want her to be the one. Want to share something with her that nobody else knows. "It was part of the first landscaping design I created on my own. And if you're into that kind of thing, a birch symbolizes new beginnings. So it's my past, but it's also my future."

Her smile dazzles me. When did I go from thinking she was cute to being dazzled by her?

"I love that," she says, and after a long moment of eye

contact, she slides her hand off my knee with a shaky little laugh. "Um, I'm going to..."

She points over her shoulder toward the kitchen, and I nod. "I'll join you."

This time she doesn't stop me from sliding my shirt on, and it feels natural to reach for her hand as we join her parents at the sliding door overlooking the backyard, where the flakes are huge and falling fast.

"Hope you're ready to shovel," Margaret tells her husband.

"No. It won't stick."

Three heads turn to look at me, and I shrug. "I work outdoors, remember? It was a little too warm today, so I don't think anybody needs to break out the shovels tonight. But if the temperature doesn't get as high tomorrow, that might do it."

Clint chuckles. "Darby, you brought home a meteorologist."

She wraps her arm around my waist possessively. "That's my man," she coos, and hey, there's that warm feeling again in my chest.

"Speaking of tomorrow." She bats her eyes up at me. "I believe we were promised lasagna."

I slide an arm around her shoulders, linking us together. "Sure, but you're coming to the store with me."

This perks Margaret right up. "Oh! I have a few last-minute things I need for Christmas dinner. Would you be willing to pick them up while you're there?"

Bad boyfriend would say no. There's-a-glow-in-his-chest boyfriend would say yes.

I say yes.

Later, as Darby and I head upstairs, I bite back a groan as I think about another night on the floor. But it's not the floor that's the problem; it's lying in the dark knowing Darby's nearby. Last night I was excruciatingly aware of the rustle of the sheets and the cadence of her breathing as I willed myself to fall asleep. Tonight's bound to be even worse now that I've kissed her.

We take turns in the attached bathroom that she shares with the bedroom next door. It's reserved for her brother, who's apparently flying in tomorrow, and I'm considering suggesting I sleep in there tonight just so I can get some distance. But when the door opens to reveal Darby in an oversized shirt, her face scrubbed of makeup and her hair in a high ponytail, I change my mind. In here with her is better.

She frowns when she sees me settling into the nest of blankets that she scavenged for me last night.

"It's really okay if you want to sleep in the bed. I don't mind."

The bed. Darby's bed. That fluffy slab of heaven, where I'd spend all night accidentally brushing against her in my sleep. I want it way too much, so I turn it into a joke, something to take my mind off the feel of her lips on mine. To turn the attraction I feel for her into another game.

"Oh, you think you could resist me if I got into that bed with you?" I gesture down my body. "You think you could resist *all this*?"

"Yes," she says dryly, although her tongue darts out to wet her lower lip before she bends to paw through her suitcase. She finds a bottle of lotion and takes it to the bed with her, pouring some into her palm and rubbing it onto those legs I can't stop thinking about.

Her phone's been shuffling through a Spotify playlist

while we've been getting ready for bed, and my ears perk up at the song that's just come on.

"Turn it up, woman."

She complies, and I start swaying to Color Me Badd's "I Wanna Sex You Up."

"This. You think you can resist *this*." I prowl forward, pursing my lips and swiveling my hips like a runway model, and she watches in open-mouthed delight as I do what I hope to God is a passable body roll.

Her soft gasp tells me it's more than passable, so I do it again, this time whipping my shirt over my head. Her gaze flies to my chest, the lotion bottled clutched in one motionless hand. I dance closer to her and lean over to pluck it from her limp fingers. She doesn't object, so I squeeze a line of the lotion diagonally across my chest, continuing to undulate to the music. Then I climb onto the bed and crawl toward her in nothing but my flannel pants. When I'm close enough, I sit up on my knees to do another body roll.

"Help me rub this in?" I slide a finger through the streak of cherry blossom-scented moisturizer and swirl it in a circle around my nipple. Her eyes track my motion, and when she kneels to face me, I realize how badly I've miscalculated things. I took my shirt off earlier to make things super fucking weird with her parents, but now that it's just the two of us, it's not weird at all. Nothing about the tension crackling in the air feels like a joke anymore.

She reaches for me, and when her fingers brush my skin, I inhale hard. Her sly little smile tells me she noticed my reaction, and she only hesitates for a beat before she presses her palm hard against the line of moisturizer, rubbing it into my chest in one firm downward motion. The movement brings her so close that our chests are practically touching, the thin fabric of her T-shirt the only thing separating us when she draws a deep breath.

"You smell like me now," she murmurs.

"Mmm." I press my nose to her neck, inhaling. She smells like cherries, the same as I do, and I dig my fingers into her hips. For the second time tonight, I'm hard as iron and aching for her, but this time I want her to know it. Even though we're not going to do anything about it, even though everything that happens outside of this room is an act, I suddenly want her to know that what's happening right now is real.

The song winds to a close, and a Taylor Swift ballad pours from her phone speaker, breaking the spell.

"That's probably enough heart attacks to give my parents for one night," she says with a shaky laugh, pulling away to turn the music down.

Shit. She thought this was another game. I practically vault off the bed now that she's made it clear that play-time's over, and once I've got two feet on the ground again, it takes a few seconds to resume normal brain functions.

"It was close, but you passed the test," I say as lightly as I can. "I guess you *can* resist me."

Barely. Her nipples are stiff points against her shirt, so if I had to guess, she *barely* resisted me. There's another good argument for me to avoid her bed. Any more encounters like that will make it hard to remember what I'm really doing here.

"I'm going to turn in," I say abruptly. It's going to be a long time before I calm down enough to go to sleep. Rubbing one out would probably help, but I'm six feet away from the object of my desire, so that's a no-go.

As I settle into my makeshift sleeping pallet, I hear

shifting on the bed and wonder if Darby's feeling the same level of frustration. She turns out the bedside light, plunging us into darkness, and Taylor warbles in the background until Darby silences her phone.

"So I was thinking."

Her voice is a little hoarse, and my body jumps to attention. "Yeah?"

"Maybe tomorrow we could watch that movie. The one that's better than *Die Hard*."

It takes a few seconds for me to remember what movies are, and then a few more to connect it to the conversation during our drive. "*The Long Kiss Goodnight*?"

"Yeah." She yawns. "Maybe it'll keep my dad awake."

"Maybe so," I say, needing the reminder about who this weekend's for. It's for Darby and her parents, her brother and sister. Not me. "Night, Darby."

"Night, Gabe."

CHAPTER TEN

Darby

Gabe's not in my room when I wake up.

His blankets are folded and stacked in the corner, but the man himself is absent. I don't waste any time heading downstairs, almost afraid of what I'll find. Is he frying eggs naked in the kitchen? Talking to my dad about cryptocurrency? Slashing the couch cushions with a pocket knife?

What I find instead are my parents sipping coffee at the kitchen table and watching a bundled-up Gabe cut back rosebushes in the backyard.

"Morning," I say cautiously. "Are you making my boyfriend earn his keep?"

My mom stands up like she's going to pour me some coffee, but I gesture for her to sit and head to the pot myself.

"He said he was bored and asked if he could winterize our flower beds," she explains.

I join them at the table. "Figures. He doesn't like to sit still. Always active, that one." And to my surprise, I know this to be a fact. I spent the past month texting with him, and we've been in each other's company nonstop for days now. It shouldn't be enough time to feel like I know someone as well as I know Gabe, but here we are.

"I'll be honest, sweetie, I can't figure this man of yours out."

My mom's frowning out the window as Gabe kneels to pull some dead, straggly weeds out of the landscaping bricks edging the flower bed.

"What do you mean?" I bring my mug to my mouth to hide my expression. This might be the very conversation I was hoping to force my parents to have, and I'm afraid my victory smile will give me away.

My dad jumps in now; clearly my parents have been discussing this.

"Well, sometimes he's like this"—he gestures out the window—"or he's asking smart questions about LLCs for his business. And then other times he's..."

"Well, he can be a bit disrespectful, sweetie," my mom says.

Yes. Yessss. They're walking into my trap. "Some-times, I guess. But he's a little younger than me."

Dad's eyebrows twitch. "How much younger?"

"Eight years," I say with a breeziness I don't feel. Thinking about our age difference still makes me uneasy, but I force a light laugh. "Age is just a number, right?"

My eyes travel past them to Gabe, face set in concen-tration as he gathers up clumps of dead plants that he's pulled from the beds. I flash hot from head to toe when I picture his impromptu striptease from last night. If him being in his twenties is what makes him extra bendy, maybe I should be grateful for that gap. That man can *move*.

"Yes, but will a younger man want to settle down?" Mom's concerned voice interrupts my thoughts. "Will he make you happy?"

Gabe's little show last night made me pretty damn happy, although I would've been even happier if I'd gotten up close and personal with that impressive erection.

That... is not what we're talking about here though.

"Gosh, I thought *you'd* be happy that I finally brought somebody home," I say with a touch of acidity.

"Well sure," my dad says hesitantly. "But someone that young, aren't you worried he'll eventually want to be with someone his own age?"

My parents are both looking at me expectantly, oblivious to my growing frustration. I wanted them to hate Gabe, not beg me to release him back into the wild for the twenty-something female population while I got down to baby-making with someone my own age. I'm gathering the courage to tell them to drop it when the back door slams and Gabe appears, his cheeks red from the cold.

"That ought to hold you until things start greening up this spring." He brightens when his gaze finds me. "Morning, babe. Grab me some coffee? You know how I like it."

He drops into a chair at the table, and I hop up to fetch him a mug, relieved to be running away from that conversation with my parents.

"If you kids are going to the grocery store, you'd better get a move on," my mom says. "It'll just get more crowded as time goes on, and they're bound to start running out of things."

Gabe takes a big swig of coffee and looks over at me. "Shall we?"

"We shall." I could definitely use some time outside of the house. After we drain our coffee, we head upstairs to get ready for Trader Joe's on Christmas Eve eve.

Just like last night, I hang out in the bedroom while he does his thing in the bathroom before slipping in to shower and dress. Once we're both decent, we head downstairs, where my mom presents us with a long list.

"A few things?" I ask skeptically.

She's unapologetic. "Christmas is an all-hands situation."

Even though I'm still annoyed about the lecture they tried to spring on me, I grab the list and we're out the door, headed to the special hell that is the pre-holiday grocery store.

"Daaaaamn." Gabe looks around the chaos of the Trader Joe's parking lot in horror. "If I die here, tell my story."

"In poetry and song," I promise.

Ten minutes later we've managed to fight through the crowds to claim a parking spot and a shopping cart, and we're dodging and weaving down the crowded aisles in search of ricotta cheese for the lasagna and marshmallows for the sweet potato casserole and bagel chips for the Chex mix, all while the Christmas soundtrack from hell blares overhead.

"I swear to God, if we have to go to a second store for one lousy item," I mutter darkly over "The Little Drummer Boy," but Gabe just laughs and swerves the cart around two forty-something men arguing over which green bean casserole recipe to use that year.

"We'll do it, and we'll be nice about it because your mom's making Christmas happen for your whole family."

His cheerfulness in the face of this hot, crowded store is humbling. "Good thing you're not actively trying to win over my parents. You'd claim favorite child status in a heartbeat."

"Good to know I'd be popular with *somebody's* parents."

He doesn't slow the cart down, so I'm left unsure of how serious he is. I link my arm through his anyway. "I'm sorry. I know you said things are better with them, but it sucks that it's still maybe not where you want it to be."

We walk a few more steps before he speaks. "Thanks. I keep trying, and they're trying too. I'm just never going to be what my dad imagined I'd be."

There's really nothing to say to that, so I try to lighten the mood.

"Have you considered showing them your dance moves?"

He turns his hottest gaze on me. "Those moves are for you and you only."

The pretty face and that growly voice? Forget it. I'm toast. I'm so toast that I almost walk into an endcap of holiday baking supplies, but he grabs my elbow and stops me just in time.

I'm about to beg him to toss me into the bed of his truck and have his way with me when a voice asks, "Darby?"

I turn around to see a blond with a severe bob smiling at me from the other side of a full shopping cart. "Oh, hey." My brain spins and spins and finally coughs up a name. "Hey, Shelly!"

"Good to see you!" My old high school classmate doesn't even try to be subtle as she checks out the man standing next to me. "And who's this? Last I heard you were single as a dollar bill."

"Wow, that's... vivid," I say through my teeth. "This is my boyfriend Gabe."

He does a little salute, and even though the move is dorky, what matters most is that he looks fucking hot while he does it.

"Wow! Good for you, girl." Shelly's gaze lingers on him a little longer than it should before she addresses me again. "Hey, a group of us are headed to Barney's for drinks tonight. You should come! Eight o'clock. Bring your man."

"Wow, okay. We'll see."

We're causing a traffic jam in the narrow aisle, so we say goodbye and head our separate ways. Gabe doesn't bring it up until we've survived the checkout line and loaded half the store into his truck bed.

"What do you think? Should we go?"

He helps me up into the passenger seat, and although most of me wants to avoid any crowded pre-Christmas bar situation, a tiny part of me wants to be part of a happy couple in my hometown.

"Maybe," I say.

In the end we do have to go to a second grocery store for those damn bagel chips, but Mom's so grateful when we get home that I'm glad Gabe guilted me into it. We spend the rest of the afternoon in the kitchen, stirring and mixing and baking and tasting. Mom pops in and out, but for the most part she's happy to leave us in charge of snacks and desserts to tide everyone over for the next couple of days. Gabe turns out to be a happy chef, and I'm equally happy to watch him work.

When the time comes for him to start putting together the lasagna, he chases me out of the kitchen.

"Listen." He grabs me by the shoulders before I go and gives me a gentle shake. "I'm going to do something terrible to make your family hate me. The less you know the better, but I apologize in advance."

"Oh." Right. Yeah. Him spending hours stirring Chex mix and rolling out sugar cookie dough isn't exactly dirtbag boyfriend behavior. He's smart to keep us on track.

For a second, I want to tell him to drop it and just be himself. And then I remember Shelly's surprise at seeing that I have an actual, living boyfriend, and irritation heats my blood. We're carrying this plan over the finish line, even if it feels dumber and dumber as time goes on. The hell with anybody who's ever pitied me for being single. I've got this brilliant deviant at my side to show them how miserable settling can be for everyone around them.

"I trust you," I say. "Sebastian's plane lands this afternoon, so maybe I'll go with Dad to pick him up and leave you to your cooking."

"Okay. Thanks." But he doesn't look too happy as I leave the kitchen.

CHAPTER ELEVEN

Gabe

"This smells wonderful, Gabe!"

Darby's family is gathered around the dining room table, and her mom's smiling at me with so much warmth that I almost stand up and walk out of the room, knowing what's about to come. But I just shrug and pick up a spatula.

"My mom learned this recipe when they were stationed at an Army base in Italy just after they were married." I start slicing into the lasagna. Steam rises with each cut I make, and I know without taking a single bite that it's perfect.

"I've been making it for years." I put the first slice on a plate and pass it down the table. "The trick is to use both beef and pork for a mix of flavors."

As I knew it would, this hits like a bomb.

"Did you say beef and pork?" Darby asks slowly.

"Yep. The perfect combo." I play dumb and keep dishing up servings.

Margaret sets her silverware down on her plate, the click somehow sounding judgmental. "Gabe, you do know that Darby's a vegetarian." It's a statement, not a question, and I dismiss it with a wave of my hand.

"Yeah, sure, but that's how it tastes best. You don't mind, right, babe?"

She's blinking at me in horror, and for a second I worry that I've gone too far. It's impossible to tell from her expression, particularly when she forces a smile. "No, it's... it's fine. There's a salad, and you made garlic bread."

"Yeah, and there's some extra sauce and noodles in the kitchen. I had a little left over, so I put the scraps in a smaller dish. There's no meat in there if it's that impor- tant to you."

Darby nods once and pushes back from the table, disappearing into the kitchen. I'm just praying she under- stands that I made her her own meat-free serving, although I'm hoping to the rest of her family it looks like she's an afterthought.

God, I feel like an asshole.

"Wait, wait, wait. So the guy who made my sister carry her own suitcase into the house also made a dinner she can't eat?"

Sebastian St. Claire glares at me across his mother's pristine tablecloth. He looks so much like Darby it's a little startling, although her pert nose and pouty mouth are masculinized on her brother's face. I just hope she never looks at me with the same contempt Sebastian's throwing my way.

"Listen, man," I say, "I just wanted to impress my girlfriend's family, so I didn't want to mess up the recipe. Darby understands."

She emerges from the kitchen with the little meat-free dish that I'd carefully set aside for her and sets it on the table. "It's fine, Seb. I want everybody to enjoy dinner."

Her assurance seems to do its job, and soon everybody's mouths are full of lasagna. I do feel a little spurt of pride that they all seem to love it, even if the compliments are grudging.

"This really is delicious," Margaret says. "And Gabe's on to something, sweetie. I think it would be good for you to put a little meat back into your diet."

Her mother's words make Darby groan. "We've been over this. I've been a vegetarian for sixteen years now and I'm not planning to change."

Now I really *do* feel like shit for blowing open an existing fight. When everyone's turned their attentions back to their plates, I shoot her an apologetic glance, and she slides me a wink as she takes another bite.

I start thinking about the recipe as I watch her chew with gusto. I've actually never made lasagna without meat, but it would probably still work with some kind of plant-based option. When I make it again, I'll...

When I make it again, I'll be making it for myself because Darby and I aren't really together. And I'm making sure of that by being a dick to her family, as we agreed.

"Did you see the chickadee at the bird feeder this morning?" Clint asks his wife.

"Birds aren't real." My reply is immediate, and Darby chokes back a laugh.

Clint blinks at me in confusion, while Margaret's focused on her salad. It's Sebastian who surprises the hell out of me. "Yeah, dude! They're battery-operated government drones."

Darby groans. "Oh no. Not you too."

I rest my elbows on the table and lean forward. "The moon landing was faked."

"Oh, totally faked." Sebastian grins at me. "You can tell in the shadows."

"It's all about the shadows!"

This is unexpected, but I roll with it. Darby told me her brother's a sweetheart of a guy, but this is the first I'm seeing any hint of friendliness. His parents clearly filled him in on how I've been treating his sister, and he's pretty much glowered at me ever since. Honestly, I like the guy more because of it. He *should* be pissed that Darby's with such an asshole.

"You boys are just being silly." Margaret spears a tomato. "Next you're going to tell me the Earth is flat."

Sebastian rolls his eyes good-naturedly. "Give me some credit. I'm a pilot. I know how globes work."

"Obviously the Earth is round," I say. "Although I am pretty sure that Dana Divine killed Mitch Cochran."

"No way. Really?" Sebastian gives a delighted gasp and whips his phone out to type in the names of America's '90s grunge power couple, and I know damn well he's pulling up one of the conspiracy theory sites that have sprouted up with all kinds of lurid plots in the twenty years following Cochran's death, none of which I actually believe but all of which I've read out of boredom.

Darby points her fork threateningly at her brother. "I can't believe you believe this stuff!"

"So does your boyfriend apparently," he says without looking up from his phone. "We're just asking the questions."

"This is my actual nightmare." She pushes her plate aside and drops her head to the table. "And it's only tolerable because I know you're both smart men who enjoy messing with your loved ones, but I swear to God if either of you explains how birds recharge themselves —"

"Power lines!" Sebastian and I say in unison, which pulls a chuckle out of Clint.

Wait. Shit. This is fun. I'm having fun joking with her brother and making her dad laugh, which is the opposite of why I'm here. So that's why I pounce at the next opportunity.

"How's your newest quilt coming, Mom?" Darby turns to me. "She's an amazing quilter. She makes them to give away or donate to auctions and things."

I scoff. "Must be nice to have all that free time since you don't work."

Inwardly I wince, knowing damn well that home-making *is* work. And the leaden silence that falls over the table tells me that I've played it just right to be the asshole yet again.

As we're cleaning up and loading the dishwasher, I overhear Darby inviting Sebastian to hit the bar with us that night, and my heart sinks a little when he agrees to come. I guess I'll have to stay on my worst behavior; I was kind of hoping Darby and I could spend an evening where we didn't have to fake anything and I could maybe convince her to kiss me again.

When she heads upstairs to change, I sprawl sullenly on the couch while her father and brother debate the Bears' playoff chances.

I want to jump into the discussion at least a dozen times, but I bite my lip and keep my eyes on my phone.

When Darby finally appears in the den dressed for our night on the town, I shoot to my feet.

"You look great."

Her hair's in loose waves around her face, and she's wearing a short skirt and tights and that fuzzy white sweater that's featured in more than one fantasy since the day we met. I'm pulled to her like she's a bag of Ruffles and I'm a chip clip, and once we're close enough, I take her by the elbow and steer her out of the room and into the hallway.

"What are you—"

"Shhh." I press a finger to her lips, then run my hands over her shoulders and down her back, resting them just above her hips. "I've been imagining how soft this sweater is since the first time I saw you. I'm so glad you packed it." I've got her pressed against the wall, and her eyes flutter shut. That, along with her flushed cheeks, tells me she likes my hands on her.

I like my hands on her too. And now all I want to do is find out for myself how that material feels against her breasts. Soft. All of it soft, I'm sure of it. I'm almost dizzy with lust, but a burst of laughter from the next room pulls me back from the brink.

Fuck. If I feel her up in the hallway, she's going to assume I'm doing it as part of our plan, when in fact I'd be feeling her up out of affection and need and that warm-as-hell feeling that's glowing in my chest again.

I take a step back, my hands falling to my sides. The urge to tell her that I like her—*really* like her—is so strong, the words catch in my throat. I like her family too. The only thing I don't like is the way they trample over her feelings sometimes, but maybe what she needs is a partner to help defuse that. Maybe what she needed all along was me—not to be the worst possible boyfriend, but to be the best boyfriend *for her*.

"What's going on in here?" She brushes her fingertips over my forehead, and that's when I realize I've been staring at her, trying to put all of this into words. But if I tell her and she laughs it off, or worse, looks at me with pity, that'll make for an awkward couple of days until we're back in Beaucoeur.

"Nothing." I take another step back, needing not to smell that cherry blossom smell on her skin before I lose my mind and kiss her. Once we're back home and away from this make-believe, I'll ask her out for real. I can be patient until then. "Just wanted to let you know that you look great. You know, before I'm on bad boyfriend duty at the bar."

Her laugh's a little shaky. "Get all that sweetness out now." She pats my cheek. "Let me grab my coat."

CHAPTER TWELVE

Darby

G abe's hands haven't left my body since he pulled me into the hallway outside of my parents' den an hour ago.

This means my body's been on high alert since he pulled me into the hallway outside of my parents' den an hour ago.

"You ready?"

He's wrapped around me like a cape as we stand in front of the entrance to Barney's. I burrow closer, pressing my back to his chest and telling myself it's because of the wind and not because I enjoy being surrounded by his arms.

"Yes." I tip my head up and back to look at him. "But do you think you can be only semi-bad tonight? I want Shelly to be a little jealous of *mah mans*."

I expect him to laugh and agree, but he frowns as his eyes travel to the wooden door where Sebastian's just disappeared.

"Think you can keep your brother busy enough not to notice?"

I grimace. "Sorry. I just don't get to see him that often, and we have lots of friends in common so I thought he'd have fun. I wasn't thinking about how—"

"Hey, it's okay." He squeezes me. "Don't apologize for wanting to spend time with your brother. We'll make it work."

Then he nudges me forward, and we step through the entrance, where we're immediately enveloped by a blast of heat and noise and yeasty, hoppy beer smells. A quick scan of the crowd shows that Seb's already secured seats at a table packed with women. Typical.

"About time," he says cheerfully when we join him. "Lauren, Kayla, Shelly, you remember my sister Darby?"

"I'm why she's here!" Shelly chirps.

Lauren, whose hair's as long and blond as ever, raises her hand in a wave. "We all made it through chem together a million years ago."

"Don't remind me!" I say with a laugh as I slip off my coat and drape it over the remaining empty chair. Before I sit, I look around for another one for Gabe, but he's a step ahead of me.

In one swift motion, he drops into the chair, grabs me by the waist, spins me around, and deposits me on his lap. To outsiders, it probably looks high-handed and presumptuous, but my brain can barely process the physical sensations of being lifted and moved and placed the way he wants me. Like I belong to him, and he's used to positioning my body for his pleasure. It's almost intolerably hot, and it must show on my face because Sebastian quickly averts his gaze to the ceiling while Lauren, Shelly, and Kayla look at me with varying degrees of awe and envy.

It's a new sensation for me, and I'm internally flustered as hell. But I play it up, draping myself against Gabe's chest. "What about you? Were you a chemistry guy?"

"Not 'til I met you," he growls in my ear, giving it a nip that makes me shiver.

Sebastian shoots to his feet. "You can have mine. I'll go get us a round and find another chair."

I just wave a hand like a queen. "I'm good here."

He scrubs a hand through his hair with an awkward laugh, clearly not used to watching me be manhandled by, well, a *man*, and turns to head to the bar, leaving the women to pounce.

"How've you been?"

"What are you doing now?"

"Is Sebastian still single?"

"Where did you and Gabe meet?"

I open my mouth to launch into our agreed-on story, but Gabe beats me to the punch with something so much better.

"This goddess right here," he says, dropping a kiss on my temple, "saved my life."

The women all murmur in interest, but absolutely nobody at this table's more interested in hearing this story than I am. Gabe's super off-script, and his eyes are alive with the barely suppressed mirth, which I know means he's about to do something unpredictable.

"I had a massively overdue library book—like years late," he says. "I'm not really a reader. Too much time at the gym maintaining all of this, you know."

He flexes the arm that's wrapped around my waist,

and if the women watching think it's impressive to see, it's even more impressive to feel as the muscles bunch and harden against me. His hand ends up resting on my side, and he starts a long, slow slide of his fingers back and forth against my sweater. Every stroke heats my blood and makes me squirm, but he just carries on as if he's not basically engaging in over-the-clothes heavy petting in front of the whole table.

"So I'm at the Beaucoeur library, there to confess my sins and offer my firstborn to pay off my debt if I have to. But the librarian at the desk takes one look at the book, and he's suddenly scared. Apparently in the years that I've had it, this has become a rare book. Very in demand. And I am in *serious trouble* for keeping it for so long and returning it with a tiny bit of damage."

He stops to look around the table, and everyone, myself included, is leaning forward to listen to whatever's coming next. He dramatically whispers the next part.

"I'd been using it to stabilize the front of my oven. Very uneven. Very greasy." Then he winks. Damn him with those sexy winks! "So the librarian's hands are shaking as he starts doing the calculations. He's getting out reference books, he's pulling out a calculator, he's summoning an old priest and a young priest."

Gabe stops and looks around the table again. "And finally he looks up, his face absolutely pale, and says, 'Sir, that'll be fifty-six thousand dollars.'"

Someone gasps. It might be me.

"And of course I can't pay that. I tell the guy that, and face gets even paler." Gabe's voice drops. "So he says he has no choice but to call in... *the enforcer*."

Everyone's holding their breath now, but he just

smiles down at me, breathless on his lap. "And then this woman here shows up."

All eyes swivel to plain old regular me as Gabe continues.

"She's dressed in black leather, head to toe. Skin-tight. *Very* sexy. Her hair's pulled back, and she's got these bright red glossy lips. She's basically the librarian domina-trix of my dreams. And she says, 'Is there a problem?' and her voice is so cold it could freeze your blood."

I'm blushing as everyone gapes at me, but I see Shelly starting to smile as she realizes that Gabe's spinning a fantasy.

"The young librarian explains to her that I can't pay off my debt, and Darby looks straight at me, straight into my soul, and tells me that the penalty for an unpaid fee of this magnitude is... *death*."

"No!" Kayla gasps, her Bambi-eyes going impossibly wide.

"Yes!" Gabe shudders theatrically, and Kayla's hand flies to her mouth. Bless her heart. "She tells me that the overlords of the library demand money or blood for this lawlessness."

Gabe's fingers are still moving over my ribs and he heads into the finale of his story.

"So I fall to my knees and beg this stern, beautiful woman for mercy. 'Please,' I say. 'I'm a simple man. I don't have much, but what I have, I'll give to you. Just spare my life.' And she lifts my chin with one blood-red fingernail" —here, he lifts his head, mirroring the action in the story— "and stares into my very soul. I'm paralyzed by her beau-tiful hazel eyes, and after the longest moments of my life, she speaks in a voice that shakes the library walls."

He pauses for dramatic effect, and after a beat, Lauren practically shouts, "Well?"

Gabe's body quakes with laughter. "Go on, Darbs. Tell them."

My mouth drops in shock that he's involving me in this madness, but no way am I letting his story fail now. I lift my nose in the air and do my best to channel this terrifying version of myself that he's created. "All right, peasant," I say. "I'll spare your life. But you *will* be in my office at closing tonight—and every night for the rest of the month. And you will not be allowed to keep your pants on for the duration of our time together."

Gabe's so delighted by my contribution that he throws his head back with a roar of laughter.

"That's right! She made me work off my debt to the overlords of the library with my body." He rocks me gently side to side on his lap, his voice dropping. "Best deal of my life."

Shelly and Lauren both giggle, but Kayla's agog. "Really?" she squeaks.

Gabe leans around me to flash her his best lazy smile.

"Nah. A mutual friend set us up a few months ago and we've been dating ever since."

The whole table explodes in laughter as Sebastian returns with our drinks.

"What did I miss?"

Lauren accepts her bottle of beer and salutes me with it. "Your sister's a dominatrix librarian, apparently."

His grin freezes on his face, and he closes his eyes briefly. "Never, ever explain that to me."

This prompts more laughter, and then the table settles into the usual catch-up stories when acquaintances haven't seen one another in years. It turns into a mix of "I knew that from Facebook" and "you did *what* when you were on vacation in Aruba?" and I'm shocked at what a good time I'm having.

As the hours pass, the bar gets rowdier with the back-in-town crowd, and when the karaoke deejay takes the stage, the place erupts in cheers at his announcement that the theme is all Christmas music, all night.

Sebastian, who's been telling his most dramatic airline pilot stories, hops to his feet.

"That's my cue to get some fresh air before I bring the house down with my vocal stylings. Anybody want to come with me?"

Lauren jumps right up and follows him out, and Gabe and Kayla brave to mob at the bar to wrangle another round, leaving me alone with Shelly.

"That"—she gestures to where Gabe's been swallowed up by the crowd—"makes me regret getting married right out of college."

"*He*"—I say pointedly, annoyed that she's talking about my fake boyfriend like he's not a real person—"was definitely worth the wait."

And he was. I didn't know it at the time, but I'm starting to think that Gabe was the one I've been waiting for all those years.

CHAPTER THIRTEEN

Darby

T he Lyft pulls up outside the dark house, and the three of us ease out of it, keeping our voices down as we thank the driver. It's well after midnight, technically Christmas Eve morning, and as a courtesy we're trying not to wake up the entire street.

It's cold tonight, maybe even the kind of cold Gabe would consider snow-sticking weather. A few flakes are already swirling on the wind, and I bounce on my toes as Sebastian fumbles with the front door lock.

"Hurry," I whine, and he just grumbles as he sorts through his keys. His mood shifted toward the end of the night, which is why I suggested we call it quits. I thought we were having a pretty fun time catching up with old classmates and butchering holiday classics at Christmas karaoke, but in the past hour or so, Seb stopped flirting with every woman who passed our table and started flashing death eyes at Gabe.

"Here." Gabe turns on his phone flashlight and holds it up to help Sebastian find the key that'll let us inside, and my brother gives him a curt "Thanks" when he locates the right one.

We tiptoe in, and it warms my heart to see that Mom's left the living room Christmas tree lit so we can navigate through the otherwise dark house.

"I never knew people did Christmas like this," Gabe says quietly. He drifts over to stand in front of the tree, the lights falling on his face and softening his strong features.

"Your family doesn't decorate?" My muscles twitch with the desire to reach for his hand, but I've been a little too free with my touches, and I don't want him to think that I'm misunderstanding why he's here.

He gently taps one of the shiny red ornaments on the branch in front of us. "We moved around so much that nobody had much use for knickknacks. We'd have a turkey and stuffing, and if we were lucky there'd be a small tree. A couple of presents, but all very practical."

"Oh no. Socks?" It's late and I'm sleepy, which means I'm not able to resist resting my head on his shoulder. So much for not touching him.

He's apparently okay with it because he wraps his arm around my waist, gliding his fingers over my sweater. I've never been so grateful for a piece of clothing in my life.

"Underwear too. Super disappointing for a kid."

"Poor little Gabe."

He pulls me tighter into his side, his strength

reminding me of what he looks like without a shirt. The memory makes me bold.

"If I play Color Me Badd, will you dance for me again?" I whisper.

He glances down at me, his eyes hot. "I think it's your turn."

"You wish."

"Yeah." His thumb slides under the hem of my sweater to brush against my side. "I do."

I forget how to breathe as his skin meets mine. And then my brother interrupts.

"I'm headed to bed," Sebastian calls from the foot of the stairs. His gaze narrows on my fake boyfriend for a moment before he looks at me, concern in his eyes. "Everything okay here?"

I have no idea what that sibling code is supposed to mean, so I just nod. "I'm planning to drink a big glass of water and fall right to sleep."

His shoulders stay tense. "Okay. Be sure to tell that fucker about our system."

I don't understand the hostility Seb's his voice, but he's up the stairs before I can ask what's going on.

"Your system?" Gabe asks as I turn off the tree lights and plunge the house into darkness so we can tiptoe up the stairs behind Sebastian.

"Our bathroom system. It's pretty simple. Lock the door to the other person's room if you want privacy, and if you forget to unlock it when you're done, the other person reserves the right to pour cold water into your ear while you're sleeping."

He escorts me into our bedroom. "Harsh but fair."

Seb's in the bathroom now, and I hear the sink turn

on, then off, then there's a short knock on my door, giving me the all-clear.

"I'll just..." I point, and Gabe nods. By the time I emerge, he's spreading the blankets out on the floor again.

I hate it, so I say something.

"What if you sleep in the bed tonight?"

He looks up from where he's kneeling. "What if you wake up to find out that I've invaded your space while we were sleeping?"

"I wouldn't mind." My pulse pounds at the thought of it, in fact.

He sucks on his lower lip in thought. Then he stands and walks over to me. "And what if I wake up with a hard-on, which I very likely will?"

"I wouldn't mind." Not at all. I wouldn't mind that *at all*.

He steps even closer. "You're saying you wouldn't mind if you woke up wrapped in my arms, with my very big, very hard dick pressed against your ass?"

"Right now," I breathe, "that is the only thing I want for Christmas."

"Fuck, Darby." He growls the words, and for a moment I worry I went too far. Then he scoops me up and tosses me onto the bed. "Let's do this."

He crawls after me and settles his body over mine. It's been so long for me that I forgot how good it feels to have someone else's weight pressing me down. I wrap my arms around his neck to hold him even closer as he kisses me.

His work on the couch last night was outstanding, but it doesn't come close to the experience of Gabe Dickenson stretched full-length against me as he tilts my chin up to devour me. His lips are firm, his tongue invading my mouth to tangle with mine. I hum my pleasure as he kisses along my jaw and down my neck.

"You even taste like cherries," he mutters, nudging my knee so he can slide between my legs. When he hears my quick intake of breath, he asks, "You good?"

"I'll be better when we're naked."

A slow, delighted smile spreads across his face. "My absolutely filthy librarian."

He works my skirt over my hips and strips off my tights. When he's done, I lift myself up on my elbows to bite his earlobe. He groans and thrusts against me, his cock rubbing against my clit through my underwear, making us both shiver.

"I'm going to touch you here, and then I'm going to lick you here, and then I'm going to make you scream. That okay?" He thrusts again, and I almost come on the spot.

"No screaming," I gasp. "Otherwise, yes."

He slants a wicked smile at me. "Oh, you'll scream."

And then he tries his damndest to make me. He moves back up my body, ghosting his mouth over mine but not quite touching my lips before running his tongue in a hot path down my neck to the deep vee of my sweater. He sucks on the skin there and groans when his hands find my breasts.

"Fuck, you're soft." He presses a kiss to my sternum and rubs my stiff nipples through my sweater and bra. Thank God it's all thin material, but I want more. I want his hands *everywhere*. When I shift to pull the sweater off, though, he stops me.

"Are you kidding? Leave it on."

He gives me another kiss through the material. "Been

thinking about this forever." He keeps traveling down to hook his fingers in my panties. "These have to go, though."

My blood feels fizzy as he strips me bare and does what he promised, running his fingers along my slit and spreading the slippery wetness over my clit until I'm panting. His fingers are calloused, not at all like the men I'm used to having in my bed. And I can't get enough. "Oh my God, Gabe."

"Not done yet." He slides his fingers down again, working two of them inside of me while his mouth descends. And then he takes his time. He takes his time licking me with long, slow sweeps of his tongue, pressed flat against me. He takes his time wrapping his lips around my clit and sucking. He takes his time, and he looks at me as he does it, his eyes hot on mine while he works me toward the best orgasm I've ever had.

And then I scream. Not *loudly*, but I definitely vocalize at a frequency best heard by dogs and small children.

"Gabriel Eugene Dickenson," I pant afterward, "that was incredible."

He crawls up and trails kisses along my jaw to my ear. "That's not my middle name."

I muster the strength to pat his shoulder. "I'll guess right the next time."

Then he collapses to the side with a groan.

"Condoms."

I groan too. "I don't have any. You?"

He shakes his head. Is it gentlemanly that he didn't assume anything would happen this weekend, or kind of insulting? Either way, it's going to keep us from getting laid. Unless...

"Be right back!"

I spring off the bed and head to the shared bathroom, stopping only to slide on the first lower-body clothing I find in our luggage corner. They're a pair of Gabe's boxers that are way too big on me, but at least they'll preserve a shred of my dignity. I approach Sebastian's door and do our old *I need to talk to you* knock: three fast, two slow, three fast. I don't have to wait long for him to appear, squinting in the bright light of the bathroom and tugging his AirPods out of his ear.

"What's up?"

Seb's a year younger than me, so we've always been close. But this is a little awkward for a grown-ass woman to ask her grown-ass brother.

"Do you have any, um, condoms?" I give him a jokey grimace, and he frowns, but he also disappears into his room. When he returns, he's holding a whole strip of them. But he doesn't hand them over.

"Are you sure you know what you're doing with this guy?"

"Yes." I extend my hand, but he still doesn't give up the goods. "What's the problem?"

He runs the hand not holding the condoms through his hair, mussing it so it stands on end. At first, it doesn't look like he's going to explain himself, but eventually he caves.

"Look, I didn't want to say anything, but..."

Unease prickles my skin. "But...?"

He sighs unhappily. "But I saw your boyfriend hitting on another woman at the bar."

"Tonight?"

He gives me a look that clearly says, *When else, dummy?*

"Oh." I wrap my arms around my stomach as if that could protect me from this gut punch. "Well, that could've been a lot of things. Where were they?"

"In the back, by the door to the alley. I think she was coming in from having a smoke."

"Wait, were *you* out there smoking?"

His ears turn red. "This isn't about me, okay? I didn't want to tell you, but he definitely got her number while you were sitting at the table waiting for him to come back. And I'm not gonna just let you go and sleep with that guy without giving you a heads-up."

My mind races. If Gabe knew Seb was around, he would've been putting on a show for him. But if he didn't, that means he really was hitting on someone else while we were out tonight.

"Did he know you were there?" I ask.

"No. I'd barely pushed the door open when I spotted them, and I watched it all happen through the crack."

It was our plan. It had to be our plan, right?

"Was she pretty?" I hate how small my voice sounds, especially when Sebastian sighs in sympathy, but a perverse part of me has to know.

"Nobody's prettier than you." His voice is soft, a brother giving shitty news to the sister he adores. "But I saw him joking with her, holding her hand, and getting her number."

Oh hell. I don't know if what Sebastian saw was real or fake, a performance or not, and now I'm off-balance about everything that just happened between me and Gabe too.

"I'm sorry." He pulls me into a quick hug, then steps back to grab me by he shoulders. "But you should dump his ass." His bossy tone splashes cold water on the warmth of our sibling bond.

"Mind your own business." I snatch the condoms from his hand and stalk out of the bathroom.

CHAPTER FOURTEEN

Gabe

I'm acting like a teenager, but I don't care. While Darby's out of the room, I strip off my clothes and stretch out on the bed, lazily stroking my cock while I think about all the things we can do tonight even if she can't find any condoms.

For starters, I can eat her pussy again. Hell, I'd happily do that all night anyway.

My dick jumps at the thought, and I tighten my fist around it, squeezing the base to get myself under control. I haven't been this excited about being with a woman in forever, and it's not only because it's been a hot minute for me. It's because it's Darby. When was the last time I'd gotten to know a woman before jumping into bed with her?

Never, probably. And I'm damn lucky that I'm doing

it with her. If my luck holds out, she just might feel the same way.

The door to the bathroom flies open, and Darby steps through. She looks positively edible in nothing but that sweater and my fucking boxers. The possessiveness that pours through me, the sense of *rightness*, is overwhelming. But when I notice that her face is stony, I scramble upright, my erection forgotten.

"What's the matter?" She's holding enough condoms to keep us busy all night, although right now she doesn't look inclined to use them.

She blows out a long breath. "This is going to sound jealous and possessive and probably a little paranoid, but did you get another woman's number tonight?"

Okay, I definitely got naked too soon.

"A woman gave *me* her number," I say cautiously.

"And did you take it?"

In a flash, I realize what's happened. "Your brother told you."

She nods, her mouth curling down at the edges. "So you know he saw you?"

"Of course! He's not nearly as stealthy as he thinks he is." I slide out of bed and walk over to her, not caring about my nakedness anymore. "That's the only reason I was talking to her."

"But my brother saw—"

"Your brother saw what I wanted him to see." And I want to punch him in the face because of it, even though this is exactly what Darby was hoping for when we agreed to this plan in the first place.

She must come to the same realization, but when she laughs it sounds sad. "It was part of the act, then."

"Yes. Yes!" I say. "Besides, what would I do with the

number of a random woman who lives three hours north of me?"

Her mouth snaps shut, and I realize about two seconds too late that this was the wrong thing to say. "What I mean is, I don't want anybody else's number. I've got *your* number."

I'm serious, but she's not listening to me.

"Was she your age?"

Her question doesn't make sense at first, and when I realize what's on her mind, that's also when I realize that it's time for me to put my pants back on. I grab them from the floor and pull them on, my movements stiff.

"I told you I don't care about that. I don't get why *you* care about it so much."

She waves her arms and then lets them drop. "I don't! It's just... I thought maybe she was actually your type. You know, younger, more confident, unlikely to drag you away from home over Christmas to make you lie to a bunch of strangers."

My type is increasingly becoming dark-haired librarians who don't see how incredible they are, but I'm not sure telling her this right now is going to help anything. So I stick with the easy truths.

"I wasn't interested in that woman. She wrote her number on my palm, and I let her because I knew your brother was right outside the door and could probably see us." I rub the heel of my hand over my forehead, trying to get this all out right. "I washed it off right away. I'm not interested in her, and I have no idea how old she is. It was all part of the act *that you wanted me to do.*"

The last part emerges a little more pointedly than I intended, but it's out there now.

"The act." She laughs without humor and jabs a finger at the bed. "Was that part of the act too?"

"Christ, no! We both wanted that, babe."

Her mouth snaps shut, and she takes a step back. "Don't call me that."

"What? Babe?"

"That's what Bad Gabe calls me." She crosses her arms and glares at me while I run through our interactions over the past few days. Dammit, she's right. When I'm on my worst behavior, I'm a smug prick who doesn't call her by her real name. And I've just done it when we're alone together, at the worst possible time.

Even though it feels increasingly futile, I try one more time to convince her that she's misunderstanding everything about tonight.

"That"—I gesture to the bed—"wasn't Bad Gabe. That was the very best Gabe I could be." Judging by her suspicious expression, Best Gabe wasn't good enough, which is exactly why I hesitate to tell her about my warm-chest feelings.

She confirms that this was the right decision by dropping her chin and addressing the floor. "It's too hard, sorting it all out. What's real, what's fake. The fact that I even have to ask means this was a bad idea. And I'm tired."

Silence fills the room as I wait for her to say more, but she doesn't.

"Do you want me to sleep somewhere else tonight?" I'm dreading her answer, and my heart sinks when she nods.

"The couch in the den should work." She says it so softly that I almost can't hear her, but the words still scrape along my skin anyway.

I snatch my T-shirt from the floor, then grab a blanket and pillow and ease out of the room, shutting the door behind me with a gentle *click*.

The next morning I wake up to the sound of shrieking children. It is undoubtedly a punishment of some kind.

I untangle myself from the blanket that got all twisted around my legs thanks to my restless sleep, and I fold it up and drop it on top of the pillow next to the couch. No need to hide it; I doubt a single person in this house is unaware of where I slept last night.

Darby must be thrilled that her plan's working so well.

"Morning." I keep my tone subdued when I walk into the kitchen to find Margaret and a younger Margaret clone sitting at the table sipping coffee while four children bounce around the kitchen, shrieking and laughing.

One of them charges me at full speed with one of the sugar cookies Darby and I iced yesterday clutched in her fist. I catch her, swing her around twice, and set her back down. She giggles as she continues her dash around the kitchen as if I hadn't briefly turned her into an airplane.

"Coffee," I say, heading for the collection of holiday mugs arrayed on the counter. I dodge another sugared-up child on my way, filling the most sedate option I can find. Candy cane-striped drinkware in hand, I join the adults at the table.

"Gabe," Margaret says, "this is Darby's older sister Celeste."

"Hi. Married to your college sweetheart, mother to

four children, right?"

"That's me." She smiles and raises her mug in salute. It's shaped like Rudolph's head, and its very shiny nose is pointed aggressively in my direction. "And those are my Christmas angels."

Two of them race by, sword fighting with empty wrapping paper tubes, and I grin at the general volume and intensity. "Cute."

"Mmm. I see what you mean," she says as an aside to her mother before turning back to me. "It's so nice that you could join us for Christmas. Is your family not in the area?"

"My parents are in Hawaii with my brother and his wife. They just had a baby boy."

Both women gape at me in shock, which enhances the similarities of their round faces and no-nonsense haircuts.

"And you're not with them for your nephew's first Christmas?" Celeste asks.

It's pointless to explain my family dynamic, that feeling of being loved but also being an outsider, so I just shake my head. "Maybe next year."

The boy child comes running past, and Celeste snags him, using the hem of her shirt to wipe his nose.

"Do you want kids someday, Gabe?"

I glance around the kitchen, hoping against hope that Darby will appear to derail this matriarchal inquisition. But I appear to be on my own. Even the kid wriggles out of his mother's grasp and darts away.

"Uh, maybe. It depends." I'm so unbalanced after last night that it's a struggle to scrape together much Bad Gabe energy, and when I look over at the four tiny siblings howling with laughter together, my mask slips. "Yeah. I do."

"That's wonderful." Margaret's eyes crinkle at me over her Santa mug. "It's lucky that you're sure, given..."

She slides her eyes over to Celeste and mouths "tick tock," and Celeste raises her brows in agreement. No wonder Darby's squiggly about our age difference; they're openly discussing her fucking expiration date. My first instinct is to shut them down, tell them I'd think Darby was spectacular if she was twenty-four or sixty-four, but that would be a supportive boyfriend thing to say, so I rally and try again.

"I mean, that's years away." I sprawl in my chair and quirk my best asshole grin. "Nobody's getting serious around here."

Margaret's mouth droops before she squares her shoulders and tries again. "So how did you sleep after your night out?"

From one sore subject to another. "Fine," I say shortly, aware that she's probably burning with curiosity about what I did to get ejected from the bedroom. I drain my mug and set it on the table. "I don't suppose you have any more gardening for me to do?"

Margaret looks pointedly out the window at the back-yard, which is a blanket of white after last night's snow-fall. "Even if there was, I think you'd struggle."

"Anything heavy I could lift or carry? Another Christmas tree to haul inside?" My muscles are itchy with the need to move.

"Ah, the energy of youth." Celeste sighs, and I grit my teeth. I didn't realize all the St. Claire women would be obsessed with my age.

There's a crash in the living room, followed by a loud wail. Celeste looks at me with pleading eyes. "Any chance you want to take these little monsters sledding?"

CHAPTER FIFTEEN

Darby

I'm awake, but I don't want to go downstairs. And it's not just because I can hear my nieces and nephews trying to shout the house down. I love them almost as much as I fear their tiny, destructive powers, and between that and the familial judgment I'm sure is waiting for me, I'm in no hurry to leave the bed.

The bed where Gabe rocked my world last night, maybe for the right reasons and maybe for the wrong ones. On the other hand, is there a wrong reason to give someone a toe-curling orgasm?

I groan and press a pillow to my face. There's a tiny possibility that I overreacted last night. And there's an even bigger possibility that I overreacted last night because I've gotten kind of used to men who say one thing but mean another and in the end are insincere assholes with no interest in sticking around. Is Gabe, in fact, the rare non-asshole, and was he serious about what he was trying to say last night?

My phone buzzes, and I push my pillow away to grope for it on my nightstand.

FAITH

How's it going there?

Ah, perfect. A Christmas Eve check-in from the woman who set all this in motion by telling Gabe that he might be able to help me with a family issue.

DARBY

Is Gabe an asshole?

Her response to my context-free question arrives immediately.

FAITH

Not in my experience.

Then again he IS a man. So.

DARBY

Yeah.

FAITH

Does that mean it's not going well?

DARBY

It was. I may have screwed things up.

I kissed him. I did a lot more than kiss him.

It was amazing by the way.

FAITH

GIRL. YES.

> But if that made things weird, just talk to him. He's got an inferiority complex and needs a little extra encouragement from time to time.

I almost ask why she hadn't tried to keep Gabe for herself, but I'd rather not plant that suggestion in case it gives her ideas. Faith is sarcastic, single, and confident, which I'm pretty sure Gabe likes. And I'm increasingly becoming aware how much *I* want to be the only sarcastic, single, confident woman in his life.

DARBY

> Okay, thanks. How's it going in Beaucoeur?

FAITH

> The usual dread before a mandatory parental visit. What doesn't kill us...

DARBY

> ...sends us to therapy.

FAITH

> LOL. Good luck. Call me when you're back in town.

"Ugh, fine," I say to the empty room. "I'll go talk to him."

But by the time I make it downstairs, it's eerily quiet. I'm starting to wonder if the household got raptured when I find my sister sitting in the living room, staring at the Christmas tree.

"What's going on?" I stage whisper. "Where is everybody?"

"My husband and our father and brother are out doing 'last-minute shopping,'" she says, busting out the air quotes.

I settle onto the couch next to her. "So they're at the indoor driving range. What about your adorable children?"

"Your adorable boyfriend took them sledding, and I'm enjoying the quiet for a second while Mom's wrapping gifts." She slumps against the couch, closing her eyes with a smile. "You know, he tried to make it seem like he doesn't like kids, but he's actually pretty great with them. I guess we'll see if he survives the afternoon."

"I can't believe you sent Ginny and the triplets off with a stranger."

Celeste cracks an eye open. "No, I sent them off with your boyfriend."

Right. My boyfriend. My totally trustworthy, totally real boyfriend.

"Gotta say, I'm impressed," she says. "I never pegged you for the himbo type."

That stops me short. "Would we say Gabe's a himbo?"

She shrugs. "He's pretty. He's enthusiastic. He's uncomplicated. Perfect fling material."

"He's not a fling," I say flatly.

She just waves a hand. "He made it clear this morning that you're keeping things casual. Good for you for scratching an itch."

"He said *what?*" For all Celeste knows, I've been planning a future with Gabe, but here she is casually dropping bombshells. Typical sibling insensitivity. "Our relationship might be new, but it's not a fling."

"Sure." She's got the smug certainty that only an older sister can pull off. "The hot younger guy you're dating, the one who works with his hands instead of his brain, he's absolutely your type. You're probably going to be together forever. Let me know when to start shopping for flower girl dresses."

"We're not..." I break off with a huff. Sarcasm aside, she's not wrong; I'll probably never see Gabe again after this week, and my family definitely won't. But my stomach clenches at the thought of him telling everyone we're not serious when I'm already wondering how I'm going to let him go once this is all over. And it's not just because he had his tongue everywhere that mattered last night, although that doesn't hurt.

I settle on mumbling, "He uses his brain." Which is true, and screw Celeste for not seeing that.

"Well," she says, "whatever you've got going on, he's definitely hot. Good for you."

Right. May as well lean into this whole mess with some younger sibling bravado.

"Very good for me. You *wish* you had some of that hot himbo action." My heart's not really in my exaggerated eyebrow waggle, but it makes her laugh, which makes me laugh, and by the time Mom queues up her holiday playlist and summons us to help wrap her mountain of gifts for the grandkids, it almost feels like a normal Christmas Eve.

We're arranging the newly wrapped presents around the tree as Harry Connick Jr. serenades us about his heart finding Christmas when our chill adult afternoon is interrupted by a commotion at the back door.

"Tristan, Kayleigh, and Madison, take your boots off first! Ginny, where'd you leave your hat and mittens?"

Moments later a horde of stomping feet and red noses come thundering into the living room to greet me with a shouted chorus of, "Aunt Darby!"

"What did you get us for Christmas?" Tristan asks,

flinging himself onto the shimmering pile of gifts, while his slightly more refined sister Madison climbs onto my lap to whisper, "Uncle Gabe took us sledding."

I cuddle her close, absorbing the winter chill clinging to her skin. Did my heart jolt at hearing her use that title for Gabe? Yes, a little. But it doesn't feel safe to examine that further at the moment. "Did you have fun?"

"It was the *most* fun!" Kayleigh shouts, joining her sister on my lap to describe their snowy adventures. As they talk Gabe comes into the room. His nose is as red as the kids', and he looks so solid and alive and happy that I want to plunk my nieces on the floor and run into his arms. When he spots me, he smiles a little shyly. Before I can untangle myself, my oldest niece Ginny catapults herself onto my lap on top of her sisters, causing them to wail as if they're being crushed to death. Nobody spares a thought for Aunt Darby, struggling to breathe under this pile of children.

"That's enough of that!" Celeste stands and claps her hands. "Rademacher children, with me. It's time for Christmas movies and hot chocolate."

Her small army whoops and storms out of the room, leaving me, Gabe, and my mother, who seems perfectly content to ignore the weirdness crackling between me and the alleged himbo.

"Gabe, there's one more box of ornaments in the basement. Could you please run down and get them, then help Darby fill out the bald spots on the tree? It's sitting by the foot of the stairs."

He and I both look at the tree, which is already groaning with orbs and stars and bears and angels, but it's not worth arguing the point. If Mom wants something decorated more than it already is, then by God, it's getting decorated.

"Yes, ma'am," he says, jogging out of the room to return moments later with a large red tote marked "childhood ornaments."

"Mom!" I groan when I realize what she's done, but she's already bustling out of the room.

"You two take care of that! I need to get dinner started. When you're done, you can help me with the mashed potatoes, Darby."

Gabe hesitates before opening the lid. "What am I going to find in here?"

"Hell. Hell is in there." I groan. "Let's just get it over with."

He pops the tote open and hoots with delight at what he finds.

"I don't think I've ever seen a balder baby." He holds up one of the many picture ornaments featuring me, Celeste, and Seb over the years. "You look like Patrick Stewart."

"Give me that!" I reach for it, but he whisks it behind his back.

"No way. I need a good look at all of these." He sifts through the small tarnished frames and globes with pictures printed on them. "Wow, your brother really had some *teeth*, didn't he?"

Oh God, if he thinks Seb's overbite is bad, I'll never hear the end of the perm I had when I was eleven.

"Huh. You and Celeste looked a lot alike when you were... Hang on. What's *this*?"

He leaps up, cradling an ornament in his hand.

"What is it?" I try to see what he's holding, but he

twists away from me, laughing the whole time. "Which ornament do you have, Dickenson?"

He holds it over my head. "This one clearly goes front and center." He fends off my attempts to block him, stretching on his tiptoes to hang it in the middle of the tree, just above my reach. I'm left plastered to his back, trying to reach over his shoulder, but he effortlessly spins me away. As he does, I catch a glimpse of his prize.

"Not the freshman class picture," I moan.

He sets his hands on my hips and holds me in place. "Oh yes. It's magnificent. The glasses. The braces. The sparkly purple eyeshadow..."

"You're a sadist."

"You're adorable." He wraps his arms around me and pulls me into his chest, lowering his voice. "Can we talk?"

I lean my head against his shoulder. "I don't want to."

"Why?" His voice softens, and I struggle to answer him. It's because I'm a coward, and I'm scared he'll tell me this has all gotten too messy to be worth sorting out. Because in the end, my sister's correct; on paper Gabe and I just don't make sense.

"Darby! A little help, please!"

My mom sounds frazzled, and I pull away, relieved for the excuse. "Sorry. When Mom's working on a big family dinner, you help her when she asks."

"I get it." He moves back to the ornament tote. "When you want to talk, come get me. I'll be finding prime spots to hang these in the meantime."

CHAPTER SIXTEEN

Gabe

I'm stepping out of the shower when I hear my phone chime with the ringtone I've assigned to my dad. Shit.

I wrap a towel around my waist and run into the bedroom, grabbing it just before it goes to voicemail. My dad calls so rarely that to not answer would feel like a failure.

"Hello, son."

Ah, yes. That's my dad, always warm and affectionate. "Hi. How's Hawaii?"

"Hot."

Okay, so much for that. "And how's the baby?"

Miracle of miracles, his voice softens just a touch. "Small."

People who don't know my father wouldn't be aware of how much emotion was packed into that one little word. It's all about the inflection and the fact that those four letters actually *have* some for a change.

"That's great. Please tell Geoff I'm thrilled for him and Vanessa."

My dad grunts. "You could've told them yourself."

And spend the holidays being reminded of how very much I'm not part of the family legacy? Not something I was up to this year, or any year for that matter. At least when I visit my folks at their Tennessee farmhouse, I'm not surrounded by a million enlisted troops at all times.

I settle on saying, "I'm sorry I'm not with you guys." This, at least, is true.

"How's your girlfriend? Are you getting along with her family?" That's my mom, talking loudly in the background.

I drop onto the edge of the bed, running my free hand through my hair to push the wet strands off my face. When my mom had pressed me on what my Christmas plans were, I'd ended up telling her I was spending it with the woman I was seeing, and she hasn't stopped asking me about it at every opportunity.

"She's..." God, how can I describe the past few days? "She's amazing. So is her family. I don't think I've made the best impression though."

Understatement, and I did it to myself. But my mom doesn't know that and rushes to my defense. "My charming boy? Never," she says. "What kind of things do they do for Christmas?"

Their Christmas traditions are different from ours in almost every way possible, although I don't want to out-and-out say that. For one thing, my mom doesn't have a bottomless supply of Christmas mugs, and my dad never let us fly down a hill on sleds in the middle of the day.

And they definitely don't cozy up on the couch to sip hot chocolate and razz Hallmark movies once the sun goes down.

"It's nice," I finally say. "I feel lucky to be included."

Unfortunately, things are so fucked up that even if I wanted to pursue something more with Darby, I don't know how I'd ever come back from her brother thinking I'm a cheater, her dad thinking I'm a semi-nudist, and her mom thinking I'm a lazy ingrate.

Christ, maybe I should've gone to Oahu after all.

"Well, we miss you," my dad says gruffly. "It's like those years when we never saw you."

I'm almost too surprised to respond. My parents never talk about the time we spent apart while I was finding my way.

"Thanks, Dad." Emotion catches in my throat for a moment before I'm able to continue. "I'd like to see you and Mom for New Year's if that's okay."

"We'd love that, honey!" my mom calls. "Bring your girlfriend."

The stairs creak, and I realize that I've left the bedroom door slightly ajar. I stand to shut it, but I'm too late, and Darby appears in the doorway, her eyes widening as she takes in my mostly naked self.

"I'll ask her, but I do need to go," I say quickly. "Merry Christmas. I love you guys."

I toss my phone on the bed and look back to find that Darby's stepped inside and closed the door.

"Sorry, I'll just—" I say at the same time that she says, "I can leave—"

We both laugh awkwardly, and I grab the towel at my waist a little tighter to make sure it doesn't go anywhere.

"The men in your family recruited me to help build

some toys for Christmas morning, so I thought I'd clean up before dinner."

"Yeah, I see that." She laughs, but it's strained. Hell, we were more relaxed around each other at our first meeting.

Her eyes drop below my waist, and like she's flipped the *on* switch, my dick stirs to life, reminding me of how much I want a repeat of the night before. But we're in a weird place, and an erection's not going to be helpful.

"Let me just get dressed."

I all but sprint for the safety of the bathroom so she doesn't get the wrong idea. I desperately want to fuck her, but I also want to joke with her, hold her hand, be a normal person around her family. Once I'm dressed, I hope I can make her understand that.

I whip off the towel, rub it over my hair, and pull on the clothes I'd packed specifically for this dinner. But by the time I emerge from the steamy warmth of the bathroom, there's no sign of Darby. The jeans and sweatshirt she'd been wearing are tossed on top of her suitcase. So she's already changed for dinner, which presumably means she didn't actually want to talk anything through.

Shit. Things really did get all fucked up last night.

I head downstairs to find the house operating at peak holiday cheer. Brassy Christmas music floats through the house, and the twinkle lights draped over every available surface—windows, banisters, mantles—cast a pearly white glow. The ornaments on the tree in the living room gleam in the low light, and whatever's been happening in the kitchen all afternoon makes my mouth water.

"There he is! Mr. Allen Wrench!"

A masculine cheer greets Clint's shouted greeting

from the den, but that's likely less from the joke and more from the glasses of spiked eggnog they're all holding.

I swing by the bar cart to pour one, then join them.

"I'm what you need when Phillips doesn't get the job done." I lift my glass in a toast that draws more guffaws from Darby's dad and brother-in-law, Aaron. Sebastian just narrows his eyes at me, which is also how he spent most of our afternoon together. The relaxed guy who traded conspiracy theories with me over the dinner table is gone, and all that's left is protective hostility over his sister.

I get it. I deserve it. But it sucks all the same.

At least avoiding direct conversation with him turned out to be pretty easy; the toys we assembled were Ikea-swinging-door-level-complicated, so the afternoon was mostly spent swearing at the shitty instructions. I briefly considered screwing up some of the assembly, but I didn't have the heart to Bad Gabe-up any Christmas gifts for children.

In truth, I don't really have the heart to be Bad Gabe anymore at all, not with the way my feelings have evolved for Darby. My stomach sours at the idea of doing more to make her family loathe me.

Maybe I'll just keep my mouth shut tonight. Better to be uncharacteristically quiet than adding to my list of terrible things I've said in this house. So I silently sip my nog until Margaret summons us to the dining room, where the table is covered in greenery, lit candles, and dishes printed with damn Christmas wreaths.

"Wow." Then all other thoughts flee my head when my eyes travel across the white tablecloth to where Darby's standing behind a chair in a red dress. *"Wow."*

I move directly to her side, everything else forgotten.

"Wow," I say again, although this time I whisper it in her ear. The dress is tight and ruffled and shows off her neck and shoulders. "Nobody should look this hot on Christmas. It's not polite to Baby Jesus."

"Back atcha." She's laughing and blushing at the same time as she runs a hand down my tie. "Mary's supposed to be a *virgin*."

Sebastian coughs pointedly as he sits down across from us, which wipes away Darby's smile, and we knock off the biblical flirting to take our seats. Time for me to keep my head down and make it through dinner however I can.

But now that I can see something other than Darby's beautiful face, I'm boggled by the amount of food on the table. "Wow." It seems to be the only word I'm using tonight.

Turkey, roast beef, and ham. Cranberries, both canned and whole. Two different dinner rolls and at least three kinds of potatoes. Salad and stuffed mushrooms and a Jell-O mold and carrots swimming in butter and green bean casserole and some kind of corn pudding. It's the most Midwestern holiday table I've ever seen.

Aaron notices my greedy stare and laughs. "I couldn't believe the spread during my first Christmas dinner either."

"I think that's why he married me," Celeste says.

"It's one of the reasons, yes." Aaron gives his wife a kiss, and that's the last adult conversation they're likely to have if their four hungry, squirming children have anything to say about it. I did my best to wear them out today by running them up and down a hill, but Christmas seems to have given them endlessly rechargeable batteries.

At the head of the table, Clint taps a fork against his wineglass to get everyone's attention.

"A toast," he says, "to the best part of the year: having our family here with us for Christmas."

Margaret dabs at her eyes as her gaze sweeps down the table. Her smile even includes me, and I feel it again, that bloom of warmth in my chest. I can identify it now, after spending time with this family. It's happiness. It's acceptance and welcome and a feeling of home.

No family's perfect, and I see the flaws in this one. But I'm so damn grateful to be at the table with them tonight. Unable to help myself, I slip my fingers through Darby's and squeeze, holding my breath until finally, *finally*, she squeezes back.

CHAPTER SEVENTEEN

Darby

Christmas Eve dinner at my parents' is my favorite meal of the year, but I haven't managed more than a few mouthfuls tonight.

It's Gabe's fault. Well, Gabe and that slim-cut dress shirt he's wearing.

"You okay?" he murmurs as he passes me the rolls.

He hasn't said much since dinner started, and when his fingers brush mine, I almost drop the basket. "Yes," I whisper back.

But actually no. I should've stayed and talked things through with him. In my defense, he practically barricaded himself in the bathroom to get away from me and my wandering eyes. He was probably scared I'd try to maul him, which was too embarrassing to contemplate. So I changed as quickly as possible and fled.

I'm regretting it now though; I don't want Bad Gabe

to come out tonight. Or ever again, honestly. It's just made everything messy. My family seems more confused about him than anything else, and my poor heart can't take much more of his conspiratorial smiles and his sweetness in private, especially with Celeste's words from this morning ringing in my head: *Good for you for scratching an itch.*

I have no idea what we're doing anymore, but I want to savor the rest of the time we do have, whatever it is. So I take a bite of cranberry salad, hoping for a peaceful dinner, when my sister commands my attention.

"Hey, Miss Librarian, isn't it time for the year-end book review?"

Ah yes, our Christmas tradition. All eyes are on me, and I turn to the small human at my side. "Okay, Tristan, let's hear it. What's the best book you read this year?"

"*Dragon Slayers' Academy!*" He mimes swinging a sword and narrowly avoids knocking over his milk.

"Oooh, that's a good one." I reach out to steady the glass. "Ginny, same question."

As it usually does, this leads to an all-table conversation about the books we read and loved throughout the year, along with favorites from years past. I'm delighted when Gabe the library-avoider admits to weeping like a baby at *Where the Red Fern Grows* when he was Ginny's age.

I pat his hand. "Don't worry. It happens to the best of us."

That's when it occurs to me that he hasn't tried to behave badly once tonight. Does he want to be done with our ruse too? I tilt my head to look at him and he meets my gaze, his eyes steady and warm.

My heart pulses, and I only look away because my

mom summons me to help clear some of the dishes so she can bring in dessert. By the time we're back from the kitchen, the conversation's shifted to what the kids are hoping to find under the Christmas tree tomorrow, and before I know it, we're forking up the last of the pecan pie and pushing away from the table with a collective groan.

"This was an amazing meal," Gabe says. Like everybody else, he looks a little glassy-eyed.

"Yep," Sebastian says, popping the P. "So many vegetarian dishes." He's slumped in his chair, staring murder at Gabe as my parents start ferrying dirty dishes into the kitchen.

I stand and pick up my plate, stacking it on top of Gabe's. "Knock it off, Seb."

"You sure like defending him." He grabs his own plate and stalks out.

"You forgot your wine!" I call after him.

Celeste snickers as she starts clearing away the wreckage from her kids' place settings. "He's in a mood."

"He needs to mind his own business," I snap.

She steadies a tottery pile of plates before speaking. "He thinks you are his business." Then she disappears into the kitchen, leaving me alone with Gabe. In the distance, we can hear Aaron wrangling the kids into hats and coats to get them out the door and into their minivan. They'll head home for the night and be back in the morning for presents, although it's likely none of them will actually get any sleep out of Santa-based excitement.

"It's not all Sebastian's fault." Gabe reaches out like he wants to take my hand, but he lets his arm fall before making contact. "I have been a total asshole."

It's the wrong time for my brother to come back into the dining room.

"Are you kidding me?" His voice echoes off the cathedral ceiling of the dining room. "You sound *proud* of it!"

Gabe tenses, but he doesn't say anything. So I do. "Stay out of it, please. You don't know what's going on here."

Seb's voice is almost pleading. "You're such a great girl, but you're settling for someone who treats you like garbage. I thought you were smarter than that."

"Hey." Gabe's voice is sharper than I've ever heard it, and it just makes Sebastian madder.

"Oh, you've got something to say about it?" His concerns for me disappears behind a sneer. "The guy who made her carry her own suitcase?"

"Enough with the fucking suitcase!" Gabe throws his hands in the air in frustration. "Yes, I made her carry her suitcase, and it physically pained me to do it. But you people? She carries every hurtful thing you've ever said to her."

We've got an audience now. Mom and Dad and Celeste have all come back from the kitchen, and Gabe's last statement makes my mom gasp.

"Hurtful things? Darby?"

"Nothing. It's fine." Explaining any of this to my parents would just hurt *them*, which is the last thing I want to do. Gabe was supposed to irritate everyone, not inflict any actual emotional damage.

But when he looks at me, his expression borders on hopeless. "You've got to be honest with them sometime. Otherwise, why'd we do all this?"

"You don't get to tell her what to do," Sebastian growls.

"Knock it off!" I say, but my brother's not done yelling.

"He"—Seb points at Gabe—"tried to pick up another woman at the bar last night. And then she"—the accusatory finger moves to me—"let him fuck her anyway."

Everybody in the room explodes at that, but by far the loudest is Gabe.

"Do not talk about her like that," he roars.

His unexpected ferocity shuts up everyone but Sebastian, who moves around the table and gets right in Gabe's face. "You shouldn't be talking to her at all! We both know what you *really* want from Darby, and it's not her personality."

Gabe's jaw works back and forth for a moment, and then he says, "You and me. Outside."

His voice is deadly calm, but his eyes are burning. And that's when I realize I need to put a stop to all of this.

"Grinch! Grinch, Gabe!" I step in between the two men, turning my back on Sebastian and putting my hands on Gabe's chest. His heart thunders under my palms. "You promised me you wouldn't fight my brother, remember?"

He glares over my head. "That's before I knew what he was like." But his breathing starts to even out, and once I'm satisfied these two idiots aren't about to pummel each other, I drop my hands.

That's when my dad wades into the whole mess. "Darby, do you mind telling us what's going on here?"

I slump into the nearest dining room chair, suddenly exhausted. The candles have burned down low, and wax is hardening on Mom's favorite tablecloth. I pick at a spot with my nail while I figure out how to begin.

"You were all supposed to hate him," I say quietly. "I

brought him home with me to be the worst possible boyfriend."

One by one, my family sinks into the chairs nearest them, looks of shock and confusion on their faces. The only person left standing is Gabe, who's got his arms crossed over his chest, every muscle and tendon in his body tense.

"Why, sweetie?" Mom asks.

I blow out a steady stream of air before speaking. Even though I know it needs to be said, I don't want to do it. Middle child. Peacemaker. The one who doesn't make waves. But where has that gotten me? Parents whose love language is smothering concern, a brother who thinks I can't be trusted to make responsible decisions about my sex life, and a hot guy who's been wearing the logo of a baseball team he hates to mess with my family. Hell, I even work in a building where people are scared to speak at a normal volume.

It's time for me to quit shutting up about what I need.

CHAPTER EIGHTEEN

Darby

Every eye in the room is fixed on me. These are the people I grew up with, whose faces I know as well as my own.

I want to bolt and never look back.

Then I look at Gabe, who gives me a nod and a tiny smile. His faith makes me strong. I can do this.

"I love you all so much," I finally say, looking from one family member to the next. "But sometimes you say things that hurt me. Like comments about being single at my age or being shocked when I bring a man home. Or"—I turn to my sister—"calling my boyfriend a hot dummy."

"What?" Gabe straightens in surprise, but I wave him off with a quick, "Later."

My dad's been listening with a hand pressed to his cheek. "Why didn't you ever tell us?"

I lift one corner of my mouth in a sad smile. "I always get over it, so why make you all feel bad? I know you're not trying to be mean." I only hesitate a little before this next part, but I might as well tell them all of it. "Did it ever occur to you that I might not want what you all seem to want for me? That I'm fine being single, and that I don't even know if I want kids? But you all push and tease and assume that you're being funny or helpful when you're really not."

It feels incredible to finally be saying it out loud, but the horrified disbelief blooming on my mom's face tears at my heart.

"Oh honey, I didn't know." She looks at my dad, then back at me. "You've always been so independent, but we hoped one day..."

"That I'd have your life?" I ask, and she nods. "I love your life, Mom. But I love it for *you*, just like I love Celeste's for her. I wish you'd trust that I'm happy with the life I've made."

"We know you're happy," my dad says, sounding a little confused and a little sad. "We just think you could be... happier."

My mom nods emphatically, but I shake my head in return. "That's not up to you. Please trust that I'm happy and"—deep breath—"please respect my boundaries when I say that the comments and advice and suggestions aren't funny or helpful. They hurt me."

She's immediately up and out of her chair, pulling me out of mine for a hug.

"I'm so sorry. You've always been such a good sport, and I didn't know how much..." Her arms tighten around me. "I never meant to make you feel that way. I feel terrible."

"Just promise you'll think about what you're saying when you talk about my decisions, okay? You too, Dad." I address him over my mom's shoulder. "No more 'way to a man's heart' stuff."

He stands to join our hug, wrapping his arms around both of us. "Okay, sugar plum. No more. You call the shots about your life."

They pull away, and my dad chucks me under the chin.

"You know we're proud of you, right?"

I inhale a little shakily. "I do. But it's nice to hear it."

"Wait." Sebastian waves a frustrated hand in the air. "Where does this asshole come in?"

He glares at Gabe, who doesn't even flinch.

"He's not an asshole," I say sharply. "He's a nice guy who volunteered to be my boyfriend this week, and then I had the stupid idea that I'd pay you all back for every time you've badgered me about finding a man."

Understanding dawns on my dad's face. "So that's why he stripped during movie night."

"He did *what*?" Celeste's eyes widen if she's picturing the whole scene.

"Just his shirt," I clarify, then turn to my parents. "The lasagna and the luggage and flirting with another girl at the bar when he knew Sebastian could see him, that was all part of it."

"I'm also a Cubs fan, Mr. St. Claire," Gabe says, moving to stand next to me. "And Mrs. St. Claire, I need you to know that your hot chocolate is the best I ever had."

My mom makes a happy little noise in the back of her throat. She really is proud of that hot chocolate recipe.

"For what it's worth, I apologize too." Gabe rests his hand on my back, rubbing a light circle with his thumb. "I agreed to help out Darby, but once I got here, I didn't particularly enjoy making all of you uncomfortable."

My mom pivots to pull a startled Gabe into a hug.

"You're a good man," she tells him.

He's so tall that he can rest his head on top of hers. "It's nice of you to say so." He pats her back a little awkwardly.

My dad approaches him next and holds out his hand. "I don't quite understand what you are to Darby, but if she trusts you, so do I."

The buzzing of Celeste's phone cuts through their emotional man-handshake.

"Shoot," she says. "Aaron's barely holding off a mutiny. I've got to go. Walk me out, Darby?"

I nod and follow her to the door, where she envelops me in a hug too. I don't think I've ever been hugged so much in my life.

"I feel awful," she says. "I didn't know it all upset you so much."

"Just promise you'll knock it off?" I pull back to meet her eye.

"Obviously." She steps back. "If you promise not to have any more interesting fights until we're back tomorrow morning."

"Ha."

"And listen," she pulls me close to say in an undertone, "I'm sorry for assuming this was a fling. The boy is obviously crazy about you."

A whisper of hope twists in my chest. "Do you think?" I whisper back.

She gestures over my shoulder to where Gabe is in earnest conversation with my parents at the dining room table. "What else would explain that?" Then with another quick hug, she's out the door.

I rejoin the family in time for Sebastian's next protest.

"Wait," he says, brow furrowed in confusion. "What about the condoms? If this is all fake, why'd you come knocking on my door in the middle of the night last night?"

This draws a strangled sound from my father, and I break the awkward silence by hissing, "Can we not do this in front of Mom and Dad, please?" I'm sure my face is as red as my dress.

"Oh," Mom says. "Oh." She looks around the room, possibly for a place to hide, then nods as if she's made a decision.

"Sebastian, your father and I are going for a drive to look at Christmas lights. Why don't you come with us?"

Ordinarily that's right up Seb's alley, but tonight he folds his arms stubbornly over his chest. "No, thanks." He's still watching Gabe like he doesn't trust what he might do next.

"Sebastian. You are coming with us." Her voice is steely, and by some Mom-magic she gets him and Dad herded to the door. But I haven't come this far to leave things unresolved with the sibling I'm closest to.

"Hey." I grab him by the elbow when he's about to follow our parents out. "Do you have anything you want to say to me?"

Seb shoves his hands into his pockets, his jaw hard. "I'm not sorry for calling him an asshole. Because he has been, and I don't like seeing you treated like that."

That's... actually kind of a fair point. But that's not what I need him to apologize for.

"What about implying that I'm some desperate crone? I'm only a year older than you, dude."

His mouth opens, then snaps shut. "Yeah, okay. I guess I kind of let Mom and Dad's comments get to me."

"It's such a double standard," I mutter, and he shrugs in agreement. Then I narrow my eyes at him. "Anything else?"

He sighs. "I'm sorry." Then his glances into the dining room. "But I'm not sorry for sticking up for you."

"When I want your help, I'll ask for it," I say. "It's enough to know that you've got my back if I need it."

Now he's hugging me too. "Always. And"—his exhale ruffles my hair—"I guess when I think about it, I was just as big an asshole to you. I'm really sorry."

"Thanks." I pull away. "I'm going to go sort things out with Gabe now. I need you to be calm about whatever decisions I make, okay?"

"Okay." He twists the knob and starts to leave. "He was actually pretty cool a couple of times."

I can't help the smile that touches my lips as the cold air rushes into the house. "I know."

When Sebastian's gone, I wander back to the dining room and collapse into my chair, drained over everything that just happened. There's one more thing I need to do, though.

I take a deep breath and turn to Gabe, bracing myself to be honest one more time. Because he needs to know how I feel about him. The *real* parts of him.

But before I can speak, he scoops me into his arms.

CHAPTER NINETEEN

Gabe

Darby doesn't speak as I carry her up the steps, but her arms wind around my neck and her lips land against my throat, which tells me I'm making the right move. Once we're in her bedroom, I set her down and look my fill.

She's marvelous. But she also just did a hard thing.

"How are you doing? Are you good?"

She kicks off her heels and crawls onto the bed while I try not to notice that her skirt gets pushed up around her thighs as she settles herself in.

"I never want to do that again." Her eyes flutter shut, and her head tips back against the headboard. "But I'm so glad I did it."

"Me too." I loosen my tie and undo the top button of my shirt. Her eyes pop open to watch my actions.

"Thank you."

I pause, then start unfastening the buttons at my wrists. "For almost punching your brother?"

A smile flickers across her face. "For sticking up for me. Nobody's ever tried to start a fight for me before."

I sit on the edge of the bed facing her. "I'm sorry about that. It's the one thing you told me not to do."

"I also told you not to hit on my mom."

"Okay, it's one of the two things you told me not to do. I can do that once she's back home if you want."

"Don't you dare." We're grinning at each other now, and I'm dying to sink into her soft body, but we've still got some items to discuss.

"So I take it you believe me about the girl at the bar last night?"

She nods, and that eases one of the knots in my chest.

"Does that mean you also believe that I genuinely wanted to be with you last night?"

Her chest rises and falls before she answers. "That's a little harder."

"Is it the age thing?" My heart's pounding at the thought that she might reject me for something I can't control.

"No. I like you just the way you are." She reaches for my hand. "I just didn't expect for us to actually..."

"Catch feelings?" Those two words feel like the biggest gamble of my life, and everything in me celebrates when she nods, her eyes not budging from mine. And then I go for it, spilling all the words that have been bumping around my chest for days.

"I liked you from our first meeting, and then I liked texting with you, and the last few days it's gotten even bigger than that. But I have to ask..."

She nods for me to go on when I hesitate.

"You told your parents that you're fine being single. Does that mean you only want a fling?"

My heart seems to pound in my ears as I wait for her answer, but she's quick to put me out of my misery.

"I was fine being single, but that was before I met you." She presses her lips together, wets her lower lip. "How could you ever just be temporary?"

Instant relief. And this next part could scare her off, but I have to say it anyway. "Good. Because what I'm feeling isn't going to go away." I press my hand to my chest, where the warmth has been expanding since we walked through her bedroom door. "I mean, I wore a tie for you tonight. It's got the fucking Cardinals logo on it."

She throws her head back in laughter. "Take it off." I comply immediately, and her eyes darken. "Keep going."

My heartbeat picks up. "Just so I'm clear—"

"My parents know a horrifying amount about my sex life after tonight, so we might as well put those condoms to good use."

Her smile is wicked, and it's all the permission I need. I yank off my shirt, kick off my shoes, and start unbuckling my belt.

"I love you in that dress," I say, "but I'm going to need it off you right the hell now."

She twists around to unzip it at the side, slithering out of it to reveal a bra and panties in the same shade of red.

"Fuck," I breathe. "Can't wait to unwrap that." Then I stalk toward her and tumble her backward on the bed to do just that. First, I unhook her bra and pull it down her arms. It's the first time I'm seeing her naked breasts, and I'm struck speechless.

"Well?" She looks at me nervously, and I surge forward to kiss her as my palms find her nipples. She squeaks and writhes and bites my lower lip, and that's when I know sex with this woman's going to be as incredible as the rest of her is.

I kiss my way down her neck and shoulder until I reach the softness of her breasts. Then I lose my cool and lunge, sucking her nipple into my mouth, stroking it with my tongue and making her writhe. I release it and move to the other one, repeating my actions until she's panting with need. I push back and look with satisfaction at her stiff nipples, wet from my mouth.

"So there's no confusion: I want to keep seeing you once we're back home." I circle my finger around one rosy peak, loving every jolt that I pull from her body. "I don't want this to end."

Her fingers clench the sheets as she tilts her pussy up, and I fucking love that she's already begging for it. "I want that too," she whimpers. "Want to make this real." This time when I lower my mouth to her nipple, I gently scrape my teeth over it, and she practically leaps off the bed.

Next, I slide down her body and strip off her panties, groaning when I find her soaked. My cock aches to be inside of her, but I have to have a taste first, so I lick along her seam and lavish attention on her clit. She tastes even better than cherries, and when she comes, she screams. Loudly. From now on, I'm only fucking this woman when we're alone so she can be as loud as she wants.

When she's done shuddering against my mouth, I stretch out next to her to let her catch her breath. While she does, I drink in the sight of her flushed cheeks, her slack mouth, her dark hair damp at the temples.

Once her breathing's evened out, I press a light kiss to

the pulse point behind her ear. "It's already real for me, Darby."

Her smile is luminous. "Me too." Then she reaches for my cock. "Let me show you how much."

It feels so good when she palms me through my pants that I know I won't last long once I'm naked. But I let her slide the button free and tug down my zipper, and I groan when she wraps her hand around my length, stroking me up and down. When she squeezes, I almost leap out of my skin.

"I'll get naked; you get the condom."

But Darby doesn't listen. As soon as I strip off the rest of my clothes, she ducks her head and swirls her tongue around my cock, base to tip, over and over, until I'm leaking pre-cum and panting with need.

"If you keep this up, I'm going to finish in your mouth," I say through gritted teeth. "But I'd rather do it inside of you."

"Okay, but mouth next time?"

I have to slam my eyes shut to wrestle myself back under control. "Christ, woman. Absolutely next time. Now come over here and ride me."

This time she does exactly what I ask, rolling the condom on and working herself down onto my cock. She sets the pace, chasing her own pleasure, reaching up to rub her nipples, then reaching back to brace herself on my thighs. Everything she does fires my blood hotter and hotter until I can't stand it anymore.

With one smooth movement, I flip her to her back and fuck her hard, lifting her arms over her head so she can brace herself against the headboard.

"Middle name," she gasps as I pound into her.

Her pussy feels so good that I've momentarily

forgotten that I have a first name, let alone a middle one, but what my woman wants, my woman gets. "Robert," I say as my vision starts to go black around the edges.

Her hands slide down to my ass, and she digs her nails in with each thrust, chanting, "Gabriel Robert Dickenson."

Hearing my full name in her raspy voice, knowing that it's as real for her as it is for me, that's all it takes. I slide my hand between our bodies, and it doesn't take long before she's cursing and coming, and I follow her over the edge, emptying myself inside of her.

We lay tangled together afterward, and I try to commit everything I've just experienced to memory. The beat of her heart, the sweat on her skin, the clench of her inner walls while I'm inside of her. I want it again and again. I might just want it for the rest of my life. But most importantly, I want Darby's sweet smile as she looks up at me from the dark tangle of her hair.

"I can't believe this all started with a joke text from Faith."

"Lucky for you." I kiss the tip of her nose.

"Very lucky for me. What do you want to do now?"

I slide out of her, already looking forward to the next time. But first...

"I'm thinking hot chocolate and *The Long Kiss Goodnight*, for starters."

She slides into my arms and rests her cheek on my chest. "Done."

"And then we'll come up here and use more of those condoms, and I don't have to be anybody but myself for the rest of the time that we're here. And then next week I want to take you to meet my parents."

She slides her hand down my arm to trace the lines of the tattoo that symbolizes my past and my future.

"I'd love that." Then she grins up at me. "Can I pretend to be a very bad girlfriend?"

I laugh softly and hold her close. "No more pretending. The only place I want to be bad is in bed."

So she pushes me back against the mattress and shows me just how naughty we can be.

EPILOGUE

A year and a day later

Darby

I t's Christmas morning, and we're all a little hungover.

Gabe and I, my parents, Sebastian, and even Celeste and Aaron had spiked our after-dinner hot chocolate the night before, all the better to savor a couple of Hallmark Christmas movies. It was the best Christmas Eve I can remember, and now we're all gathered around the tree in our pajamas, nursing coffee and watching the Rademacher children destroy their gifts.

"Did you see the conspiracy about Mattress Hut?" Gabe asks Sebastian, who lights up brighter than the tree.

"No! Tell me everything."

The rest of the room groans and boos them. "No conspiracies on Christmas morning!" Celeste orders.

"Spoken like a member of the Illuminati," Gabe whispers to Seb, and I snort-laugh at their nerdiness. Then Gabe stands up. "Coffee refills?"

He collects everyone's empty mugs, and while he's gone I scope out the rest of the tree. I know the rectangular box in the corner has a pair of flannel Cubs pants for Gabe from my parents. I'm terrified to think what Sebastian might've gotten him but have a sneaking suspicion it'll be along the lines of the "Birds aren't real" T-shirt Gabe bought for him.

What really interests me is the tiny box I know Gabe's been carrying in his pocket all week. It disappeared for a while, and now it's wrapped in shiny red paper and tucked into a lower branch of the tree. My mom's been misty-eyed every time she looks at me, and my dad's been unusually quick with the fatherly backslaps to Gabe. Also, Celeste has been openly asking me what colors I prefer in formal dresses for little girls.

My whole future's wrapped up and waiting for me, and when Gabe comes back into the room balancing a tray, my heart swells so much it's almost painful.

He circles the room before taking his place next to me on the couch and sets his Rudolph head mug on the table in front of him so he can wrap me in his arms.

"I love you," he murmurs.

"I love you too," I murmur back.

A few minutes later when he hands me that tiny box, it's the easiest yes in the world.

BONUS EPILOGUE

This bonus epilogue was originally available
only to newsletter subscribers.
It takes place the Thanksgiving before the first epilogue.

Gabe

I t's 4 a.m., and the St. Claire house is dark as I creep down the stairs carrying my shoes. Once I'm on the main floor, I tiptoe down the hall, barely avoiding a collision with an end table thanks to the glow of the angel-shaped night light plugged into the wall.

"I knew you weren't in it for the long haul."

I wish I could say that the voice slithering down the dark hallway didn't make me squeal like a small child, but it did. A moment later, Sebastian St. Claire steps into view, barefoot in flannel pants. He's got a playful smirk on his face. We may have started off rocky, but after eleven months of family events and a few long sibling weekends, we've gotten tight.

"Keep it down, dude," I hiss. "You'll wake everybody up."

He glances upstairs. "They're all sleeping off their turkey. Except you, apparently." He lifts his brows as he watches me slip on my shoes. "Headed somewhere?"

"The mall."

His brows are at his hairline now. "Today? Are you crazy?"

"Crazy for your sister," I reply. "She wants this fancy kitchen mixer... thingy. And it's on some kind of special Black Friday sale this morning, and..." I shrug. I love Darby enough to brave the Friday-after-Thanks-giving mall. The lift and fall of my shoulders speaks volumes.

Seb's face splits into a grin. "Cool. I'll be your wing-man. Give me a second to get dressed."

I've barely gotten my coat zipped up by the time he's back in jeans and a hoodie.

"Dang. Do pilots practice getting dressed in the dark or something?" I ask.

He grins as he grabs his own coat from the hook. "Or something. Let's go."

"This was a mistake."

At my horrified whisper, Sebastian claps me on the back. "Nah, you've just gotta channel your competitive spirit. Let's see..."

He spins in a complete circle once, then again, his eyes scanning the hoards crowding the aisles and massing around the check-out counters of the department store in Woodfield Mall.

On his third revolution, he stops in his tracks, his nose twitching like a bloodhound's.

"Housewares this way," he announces, taking off and leaving me to weave through the press of bodies to keep up with him. I trail him through half the store until he slams to a halt in front of the displays of stand mixers. He casts wary glances at the shoppers circling the display, clearly a veteran of doorbuster sales skirmishes.

"Done this before?" I ask.

"You've met my family, right?" He pretends to buff his nails on his coat. "Stick with me. I'm a veteran of decades of pre-Christmas shopping expeditions."

Good lord, the St. Claires love the holidays.

This particular St. Claire rubs his hands together as we study the gleaming mixers on display. "What color?"

Seb looks ready to throw elbows to get me what I want, but my brain stalls. There are so many options. Darby told me she always wanted one of these fancy mixer boys, but she didn't specify a color. And I had no idea there were so many to choose from.

There's silver. Black. Peach. Butter-yellow. Fire-engine red.

A woman in a light-up reindeer sweatshirt apparently gets tired of my indecision and shoves between us with a muttered, "'Scuse me." She snatches up a box with an all-white model and chucks it into her overloaded cart before trundling off.

"Wait, was that the last white one?" I check the boxes stacked behind the display. We got here just as the sale was starting, and the supply's already dwindling.

"She wouldn't want that color anyway," Sebastian

says as he sorts through the choices that remain. "This one, maybe?" He points to a model near him, but I shake my head.

"She doesn't like hot pink."

Seb glances up at me in mild surprise, and I shrug. "She tried nail polish that color a few weeks ago and left it on for 10 minutes before scraping it all off."

"Ooookay," he replies. "What about yellow? It'll match her kitchen."

He's right; it does. But that's why I hesitate.

"Actually..." Should I tell him? I should tell him. "I don't think she'll be in that house much longer."

Another surprised look, and this one makes me grin in response.

"I'm going to ask her to marry me," I say in a rush, my stomach in nervous knots. "I'm hoping we can pick a new house to move into together."

"Dude!" Sebastian's whole face lights up. "That's incredible!" He grabs my shoulder and squeezes. "She'll be thrilled."

"Hope so," I say, my nerves easing. Seb's the first member of Darby's family I've told, and I was a little afraid he'd think it was too soon. Or worse, that he still had negative thoughts about all the shitty things I did last Christmas. But he's beaming at me, the hunt for the perfect mixer momentarily forgotten.

"When are you gonna do it?"

A shopper clips my shoulder with the end of a rolled-up rug he's hauling to the check-out, and I grunt and shuffle forward.

"Not sure yet, but maybe over Christmas?"

"Yes!" Sebastian pumps his fist. "The whole family'll love that." Then his smile dims, and thanks to a few recent conversations over drinks, I have a good guess as to why.

"Still haven't found your perfect girl?" I step closer to the display to avoid the line of people snaking back from the shoe department.

"Nah." Sebastian shoves his hands in his pockets, trying to sound casual even though he's been on a pretty serious dating spree since Darby and I got together. Something about him not wanting to be the last single St. Claire. "It's bleak out there."

I nudge his shoulder. "Somewhere there's a girl who's willing to put up with your ugly face and boring job."

He snorts. "Well she's definitely taking her time finding me." But his grin is back in place, and he snaps his attention back to bargain-hunting. "How about blue?"

I take in the mixers he's pointing to. How in the world are there so many different shades?

"Hmm." I rest my hand on the robin's egg blue model. It's pretty. It's a color Darby likes. I'm ready to say yes when a model at the very end catches my eye. "It's that one," I say decisively.

Sebastian follows my gaze to the bright green mixer almost hidden behind the sage and the salmon ones. "Ooh, that's nice," he agrees.

"It is." I move closer. It's cheerful. Bold. It's a Christmassy shade to remind us of when we fell in love, but it's a playful choice for the rest of the year too. "This is the one." We can decorate a new kitchen around that shade. Build a home together starting with this and the engagement ring I picked out last week.

"On it." Sebastian moves like a machine, shifting boxes until he holds up a green one in triumph. "Success!" Then he glances around at the shifting crowds and tucks it defensively under his arm. "Let's take it and run."

We're back home an hour later, and the St. Claire household's finally starting to wake up.

"Where have you two been?" Darby's eyes flit between me and Sebastian when we tumble in through the back door, grins on our faces and to-go coffee cups in our hands.

"Elf stuff," Seb says as he sets down the box of donuts we picked up on our way back to the house.

Darby ignores the donuts and turns her attention to me, excited curiosity all over her face. "Elf stuff?"

She's in a ratty polka-dot robe and a bedraggled ponytail, and she's never looked more gorgeous. I stride over to her and kiss her senseless, bowled over as always by how much I love her.

"Yeah." I bend close to whisper in her ear. "Just call me Santa's little helper, here to make all your dreams come true."

"Too late," she whispers back. "You already have."

Sebastian St. Claire has his own Christmas romance when he embarks on a snowy cross-country road trip with his disastrous hook-up from the night before. Read My Holiday Hookup Road Trip *now!*

ACKNOWLEDGMENTS

I had *the most fun* writing this book, which sprang from the usual unhinged conversations in the Geriatric Friendship Cult. Many thanks to Skye Malone, Holly Ashby, Tanya Melendez, and the Disco Vinnies for cheering me on along the way.

ALSO BY SARA WHITNEY

Cinnamon Roll Alphas

Tempting Heat

Tempting Taste

Tempting Talk

Tempting Lies

Tempting Fate

Hot Under The Mistletoe

My Fake Bad Boyfriend

My Holiday Hookup Road Trip

My Not-So-Secret Santa

Standalone Novellas

Game On

Ghosted

ABOUT THE AUTHOR

 Sara Whitney worked as a journalist and film critic before she earned her Ph.D. and entered academia. She divides her time between professoring, authoring, and entertainment reporting, and she almost certainly has an opinion about your favorite TV show.

Sara writes her sexy, sunny romance novels in Illinois, where she's surrounded by books, cats, half-full coffee cups, and practically empty bags of Swedish Fish.

Keep up with the latest news by subscribing to Sara's mailing list at **www.SaraWhitney.com/VIP** or use your phone's camera to scan the code below:

Made in United States
Orlando, FL
13 November 2023

38914246R00104